Stefanie. Kristin. Raposa.

Stefanie. Kristin. Raposa.

FIFTY STORIES for 6 YEAR OLDS

FIFTY STORIES
for 6
YEAR OLDS

Edited by
Marie Greenwood

Illustrated by
Hilda Offen

GALLERY BOOKS
An Imprint of W. H. Smith Publishers Inc.
112 Madison Avenue
New York City 10016

ISBN 0 8317 3276 8

FIRST AMERICAN EDITION 1989

PRINTED IN YUGOSLAVIA

ACKNOWLEDGEMENTS

For permission to include copyright material,
acknowledgement and thanks are due to the following:

Brian Patten and Unwin Hyman Ltd for *The Giraffe Who Saw to the End of the World*
from 'The Elephant and the Flower'

Linda Allen and Deborah Rogers Ltd, Literary Agency, for *Mrs Simkin's Bathtub*

Joan Aiken and Jonathan Cape Ltd for *The Patchwork Quilt* and *The Baker's Cat*

Anita Hewett and The Bodley Head for *Lizard Comes Down from the North*
from 'The Anita Hewett Animal Story Book'

The following are reprinted by permission of Faber and Faber Ltd:

Tim Rabbit and the Scissors by Alison Uttley
from 'The Adventures of No Ordinary Rabbit'

The Fairy Ship by Alison Uttley from 'John Barleycorn'

How the Whale Became by Ted Hughes from 'How the Whale Became and Other Stories'

The Ossopit Tree by Stephen Corrin from 'Stories for Five Year Olds'

All other stories in this book are retold from traditional sources
by Nora Clarke and Linda Yeatman and in this version are © Grisewood & Dempsey Ltd
except *The Selfish Giant* by Oscar Wilde which is reprinted in the original version.

CONTENTS

THE THREE BROTHERS

There was once an old man who had three sons. He loved them very much and they lived happily together in a comfortable house.

"Who shall I give this house to when I die?" the old man wondered. "I must be fair to each one because all three have been so kind to me. I have nothing of value, except my house, so I think I shall sell it and then divide the money I am given for it into three parts."

He called his sons to him and explained his idea.

"Oh no," they said. "Your father and your grandfather lived in this house. They were happy with their families here, the same as we are. Please don't sell it."

"Of course I'd rather stay here," and the father smiled at his sons. "But I need the money to give you a share of all that I have. How else can I do that?"

The eldest son looked very thoughtful.

"Listen, everybody, I have a plan," he said. "Why don't the three of us leave home for one year and learn to do something we really like. When we return, father will give us a test then he can decide who has learnt to do his work the best. Whoever wins will get the house so that one of the family will still live here."

"What a splendid idea," the other sons said at once. "If father agrees, let us think about the work we'd like to do."

The father did not want his sons to go away but he agreed to this plan.

"I love horses and I want to be very strong," the eldest son said, "so I think I'll be a blacksmith."

"I like using my hands and I'm very good with scissors and a razor," said the second son. "What about learning to be a barber?"

"I'm quick and light on my feet," the youngest one laughed as he twirled around. "I'd like to use a sword really well. I'm sure

I can become the best swordsman in the world!''

So on a lovely morning in June they hugged their father and gave him a fond farewell.

"We'll return home on Midsummer's Day a year from now," all three promised as they set off together into the country.

When they had walked a good way they came to a crossroads. The eldest son said: "Here we must part; but a year from today we will come back to this spot, and in the meantime we must try and learn our chosen trade as well as we can." The three brothers shook hands with each other and each set off down a different road.

The months passed slowly for the father because he was lonely without his sons at home but they were so busy that the time went by very quickly for them. They learnt their trades so well that in March they began to work on their own.

First the king heard such a lot about a new and clever blacksmith that he ordered him to shoe the royal horses.

Then all the noblemen rushed to visit the second son who cut hair and trimmed beards in very smart styles.

The third son still wanted to be the best swordsman so he had to practise very hard and in the end many people were flocking to see a wonderful young man using a sword.

The three of them remembered their promise even though they were so busy and on Midsummer's Day they met together at the crossroads, and having welcomed each other, set off towards their father's home. The old man rushed out to meet them as soon as he saw them coming, he was so delighted to see his dear children.

"Welcome, my sons," shouted the father. "I've missed you very much. Come, let us enjoy the feast I've prepared for you and then we can decide who has learnt his trade the best. I am looking forward to seeing what my children have learnt while they have been away from me."

Each son was sure he was the cleverest and would win the house so they didn't argue but ate plenty of the delicious food. Then they went for a walk together across the fields to think about the tests which they had to do.

Suddenly a rabbit came running towards them. In a flash, the barber pulled out a mug and soap and he whipped up a lather. Then as the rabbit scuttled past, he dabbed soapy bubbles on its chin and shaved off its whiskers with a razor. It happened so quickly that the rabbit didn't even notice what had happened and it rushed on.

"This must be the best and fastest barber in the country," the father thought, "he must win the house."

They walked on for a little while when all at once a gnat buzzed near their heads. Instantly the blacksmith seized his tools and fitted tiny horseshoes onto the insect. He fastened them with gold pins without hurting the gnat which went on flying and buzzing around.

"What a wonderful blacksmith!" The father felt very proud. "Surely *he* must have the house."

Just then it started to rain but before a single drop could touch the youngest son's head, he had drawn his sword. He swung it backwards, forwards and all around him, beating every raindrop away. The rain fell heavier and heavier. Soon everybody was soaking wet – except for the swordsman. His sword whirled and flashed but his arm did not get tired and his clothes stayed completely dry. Not one drop of rain fell on him for his sword had beaten them away.

"This is wonderful!" exclaimed the father. "I'm very pleased with such an amazing blacksmith and the fastest barber, but truly the swordsman is the best. To him therefore, I must leave the house."

"I agree," said the eldest son at once, who was a fair-minded person.

"We are very proud of you," the second son told his brother generously.

"Thank you, dear father and my brothers," said the youngest one, "but there is room for everybody surely. Please don't go away."

So they all stayed together in the old family house and they remained good friends all their lives.

CINDERELLA

There was once a gentleman who lived in a fine house with his pretty daughter. His kind and gentle wife had died, so the gentleman married again. His new wife was not at all kind or pretty. She had been married before and had two daughters who were known, behind their backs, as the Ugly Sisters.

Although they had no reason to be unkind, the two sisters were horrid to their new stepsister. They ordered her about, scolded her and made her do all the work in the big house. Her clothes became ragged and thin and far too small. "We've no money to spare for you," the two sisters would laugh. The poor girl was always cold and tired. In the evenings she would rest on a stool close to the fire, almost in the cinders and ashes.

"Cinderella. That's the perfect name for you," jeered the stepsisters when they saw her trying to keep warm. Cinderella had too sweet a nature to complain, and her father was much too busy to notice how badly his new wife and his stepdaughters treated her.

The king and queen of their country had a son who was not married, and they planned a big ball for this prince in the hope that he might find a bride. Invitations were sent to princesses in the neighbouring countries and to all the big houses in their own country. When a large invitation card to the royal ball arrived at Cinderella's house, there was a great flurry of excitement. New dresses were chosen for the Ugly Sisters and their mother, and nobody talked about anything except the ball.

"I am sure the prince will fall in love with me," said one sister, smiling at herself in the mirror.

"You silly fool," said the other, pushing her aside. "He won't be able to resist falling in love with me. Just think, one day I could be the queen," and she pretended she was the queen already as she ordered Cinderella to get another pair of shoes for her to try on. No one thought of asking Cinderella if she would like to go to the ball. They scarcely even noticed her as they rushed around trying on different wigs, fans and gloves to go with their new ball dresses.

At last, the day of the ball came, and Cinderella worked harder than ever, helping the Ugly Sisters and her stepmother to get ready. They quarrelled with each other all day, and by the time the carriage drove away to the king's palace, with all the family in it, Cinderella was glad to have some peace. But as she sat on her stool by the fire she could not help a tear falling onto the ashes for she wished that she could have gone with them.

Suddenly she blinked as she found she was not alone. A beautiful lady stood before her with a silver wand in her hand.

"Cinderella, I am your fairy godmother. Don't cry but tell me what those tears are for?" At her kind words, Cinderella dried her eyes,

"I wish, oh how I wish, I could have gone to the ball too."

"So you shall," said her fairy godmother, "but first we have some work to do."

"Oh no," sighed Cinderella, "not work, not more work."

"Yes, work!" said her godmother, "For if you are to go to the ball, I cannot send you as you are. But we will do it together. First, fetch me the largest pumpkin you can find in the garden."

Cinderella fetched the largest pumpkin she could see and in a flash and wave of her hand, her fairy godmother had turned the pumpkin into a gleaming golden coach.

"Now we need a few horses," said her godmother. "Look in the mouse trap and see if there is anything there we can use."

Cinderella ran to the larder where there were six mice running around in a cage. Once more Cinderella watched her godmother wave her wand. There, suddenly, harnessed to the coach, were six shining dappled horses, stamping their feet, impatient to be off.

"Those horses need a coachman," decided the godmother. "Look in the rat trap, Cinderella." There were three rats in the trap and as the godmother touched the largest rat with her wand, it disappeared. But now up in front of the coach sat a fine, plump, whiskery coachman in smart uniform.

"Go and look behind the water barrel, Cinderella," said her

godmother, "and see if you can find something there we can use for footmen."

Cinderella ran to the water barrel and brought to her godmother two lizards. At the wave of her wand they were transformed into splendid footmen who jumped up on to the back of the coach as if they had done this all their lives.

"There now, Cinderella, your coach is ready," said her godmother with a smile. "Soon you will be able to go to the ball."

"How can I go like this?" sighed Cinderella, looking down in despair at her ragged clothes and bare feet. But even as she hung her head, her godmother touched her with her wand and her rags turned into a shimmering gown. Cinderella gasped. On her feet

she was wearing the prettiest pair
of glass shoes she had ever seen.

As Cinderella stepped into the
coach her godmother gave her
a strict warning. "The magic will only last until midnight, and
then everything will return to what it was before. Be sure you
leave the ball before midnight, Cinderella."

When Cinderella's coach arrived at the palace the word went
round that a beautiful lady had arrived in such a splendid coach
that she must be a princess. The prince himself came down the
steps to greet her. Stunned by her beauty he wanted to dance with
her at once and led her straight to the ballroom. The other guests
fell silent and the musicians stopped playing as everyone gazed in
wonder at the lovely girl with the prince. Even the king sat up and
remarked to the queen that it was a long time since he had seen
such a pretty girl. The prince signalled to the musicians to play
again and then took Cinderella in his arms and danced with her.

All evening the prince stayed at Cinderella's side. No one
knew who she was. Not even the Ugly Sisters recognized her, even
though Cinderella spoke to them and gave them some of the
sweets the prince had given her. Cinderella herself was so happy
she did not notice how quickly the time was flying by.

Suddenly she heard the clock strike the first stroke of
midnight. With a small cry she escaped from the prince and ran
towards the door of the palace. The prince lost sight of her
although he followed as closely as he could. As the great clock
continued to strike Cinderella ran down the steps, and into the
courtyard. She did not even have time to pick up one of her shoes
that came off as she ran.

The prince questioned everyone carefully but no one had seen
the beautiful lady leave. The guards at the gate swore the only
person who had gone through was a young raggedly-dressed girl.
No one noticed the pumpkin in the corner of the courtyard or some
mice, a rat and a pair of lizards that slunk into a dark corner.
However the prince did find on the steps a glass shoe, and he
recognized it as one of the elegant shoes the mysterious and lovely

lady had worn.

The ball went on for many more hours so Cinderella reached home before her family, although she had to walk. The next day they could talk of nothing but the beautiful girl who had captured the prince's heart, of how she had disappeared so suddenly and how no one knew her name. The Ugly Sisters even boasted to Cinderella how lucky they had been to talk to the stranger and how kind she had been to them. Cinderella smiled as they talked but never said a word.

Later that week a proclamation was given from the palace that the prince was looking for the guest who had worn the glass shoe. His servants would tour the country with it until they found the lady whose foot it fitted and the prince would marry that lady. The prince, unable to think of anything except the lovely lady, travelled round with his servants but time and again he was disappointed as the shoe failed to fit any lady's foot.

At last they came to Cinderella's house. The Ugly Sisters were waiting.

"Let me try first," cried one, holding out her foot, and pushing as hard as she could to squeeze it into the shoe. But however hard she tried, she could not get the shoe on. At last she gave up and laughed at her sister's efforts as she, too, squeezed and pushed to get her foot into the tiny glass shoe. When she had failed, the palace servants asked if there were any more young ladies in the house, at which Cinderella stepped forward.

"You!" laughed and jeered the Ugly Sisters. "You were not even at the ball."

"The prince wants all young ladies to try," said one of the royal servants sternly.

Cinderella put her foot out and the glass shoe slipped on as though it had been made for her. Then there was a gasp of surprise as Cinderella drew from behind her back a second shoe which she put on her other foot. The prince came forward and held out his arms, and at the same moment the fairy godmother appeared and touched Cinderella with her wand. Instantly her ragged clothes changed into a beautiful dress, and everyone stared in amazement as Cinderella became the lovely stranger at the ball.

The prince was overjoyed to have found his beautiful lady at last and he asked Cinderella to marry him at once. Cinderella was filled with happiness and said there was nothing she would like more.

The Ugly Sisters felt guilty about their past behaviour and begged Cinderella to forgive them for their unkindness and Cinderella was more than happy to agree.

There was a fine royal wedding for Cinderella and her prince which everyone enjoyed. Some months later Cinderella found husbands at court for both the Ugly Sisters. Everyone agreed that Cinderella was as kind as she was beautiful.

The prince loved Cinderella dearly and they lived happily together for a long, long time.

THREE BILLY GOATS GRUFF

Once upon a time there were three goats who all lived together. They were known as the Three Billy Goats Gruff. All of them had curly horns and tufted beards. They lived in a village where there was not always enough food for them, so they loved to cross over a wooden bridge to the other side of the valley to munch the rich grass in the meadows there.

A deep river ran under the bridge, and beside the river and under the bridge lived a fierce troll. He had a long nose, huge eyes and big teeth. He was an ugly, bad-tempered troll and, more than anything, he hated people or animals to cross the bridge. If he could catch them, he would eat them. The three billy goats had to try and get across to the valley without disturbing the troll, if they possibly could.

One day the troll was lying under the bridge when he heard the sound of steps TRIP TRAP, TRIP TRAP on the wooden planks above him.

"Who goes there?" roared the troll angrily.

The smallest Billy Goat Gruff was on the bridge, and he called out in a small frightened voice,

"It is only I, the little Billy Goat Gruff."

"Then I will eat you for my dinner," roared the troll.

"No, no," pleaded the little Billy Goat Gruff. "Let me cross

over and eat the grass on the other side and I will grow fatter. My brother, the middle-sized Billy Goat Gruff, will be coming along soon. Why don't you wait and eat him?"

"Very well," grumbled the troll, and settled down under the bridge to wait for the middle-sized Billy Goat Gruff.

Before long, he heard TRIP TRAP, TRIP TRAP on the wooden planks above him.

"Who goes there?" roared the troll.

"It is I, the middle-sized Billy Goat Gruff," replied the goat in a middle-sized voice.

"Then I shall eat you for my dinner," roared the troll.

"I think," said the middle-sized Billy Goat Gruff, "you would do better to wait for my brother, the big Billy Goat Gruff. He will make a much better dinner, and meanwhile I shall be able to get fatter in those meadows over there."

"Very well," huffed the troll. He heard the middle-sized Billy Goat Gruff go TRIP TRAP, TRIP TRAP over the bridge and settled down to wait for the big Billy Goat Gruff.

Before long the big Billy Goat Gruff came along. The troll heard his hooves on the bridge above him. This time the TRIP TRAP, TRIP TRAP was loud and heavy.

"Who goes there?" roared the troll.

"It is I, the big Billy Goat Gruff," called the big goat in a big gruff voice and he sounded almost as fierce as the troll.

"Then I shall eat you for my dinner," bellowed the troll.

"Oh no you won't," replied the big goat, "for I have sharp horns and will kill you first."

The troll was so angry that he leapt out from underneath the bridge and attacked the big Billy Goat Gruff. But the big goat was waiting for him and stood firm, with his head down and his horns ready. The troll was tossed in the air and fell with a tremendous SPLASH far down into the deep river where he drowned.

The big Billy Goat Gruff went on his way to join his two brothers, TRIP TRAP, TRIP TRAP over the bridge and into the meadows. Now every morning and evening they could come and go over the bridge as they pleased, and I'm sorry to say that they all grew very fat indeed.

THE FISH
AND THE RING

A long time ago in the Northlands there lived a rich Baron who knew all about magic. On his little boy's fourth birthday he wanted to find out what his son would do when he was a man. He read his Book of Magic and he was very angry when it told him that his son would marry a poor girl who had just been born nearby.

"I'll see about that," he roared. "Bring me my horse!" and he rode off in a furious temper. Soon he reached a little house and saw the baby's father sitting outside looking very miserable.

"What's the matter?" the Baron asked.

"Well, we're very poor," said the man. "It was very hard to buy enough food for five children so I don't know how I'll manage to feed six!"

"Perhaps I can help." The Baron got off his horse. "Let me have the new baby and I'll take care of her."

"Thank you, you are very kind," said the father. "Please look after her well."

The Baron promised he would take care of her, then he rode away with her on his horse. But when he came to a river bank, he threw the little girl into the water and galloped back to his castle.

However, the baby's clothes filled with air and she floated on the water until a fisherman spotted her and pulled her to safety. He was sorry for the baby and looked after her in his house. Time passed and she grew into a kind and beautiful young lady.

One day the Baron and his friends were out hunting and as they were tired and thirsty they stopped at the fisherman's house.

"Ho there! Can you give us a drink?" the Baron shouted.

"Only water, sir," the fisherman said and he called to his daughter to bring out the water jug. She obeyed at once and the hunters gasped in surprise at her beauty.

"Well now, Baron," said one of them, "you have magic powers. Tell us who will be this beautiful girl's husband."

20

"Oh, a fisherman or a farmer, I expect," he replied scornfully, "but I'll look in my Book of Magic to please you. Come closer, my girl and tell me when is your birthday?"

"I'm afraid I don't know," said the girl. "This kind fisherman found me floating in the river fifteen years ago and he rescued me and gave me a home."

At once, the Baron guessed who she was. Quickly he told his friends that it was time to be going but after a short time he rode back alone and spoke to the girl.

"I've been thinking that such a clever girl like you should be given the chance to make her fortune. I'd like to help you so take this note to my brother in the city. He will know what to do."

Of course the young girl was overjoyed, but this is what the Baron's letter said:

"Dear Brother,
          The bearer of this letter is wicked. Kill her at once.
                    Your affectionate brother."

The girl set off on her journey and on the way she rested for the night at a small inn. While she was asleep a band of robbers attacked the inn. They searched the girl's belongings but she had no money, only the Baron's letter. They tore it open and read it. "How terrible," they whispered, "she is too young to be killed."

"I have an idea," said the robber-captain. "Don't say a word to the girl for she will still have a letter to take to the city tomorrow!"

He took pen and paper and wrote the following:

"Dear Brother,
          The bearer of this letter is quite lovely! Marry her to my son at once.
                    Your affectionate brother."

Next day the girl walked to the city. She found the Baron's brother easily and handed him the letter. He read it carefully and smiled. "My nephew, the Baron's son, is staying with me at the moment. I'll give orders for the wedding to take place at once."

21

So the girl and the Baron's son were married the same day.

A little later, the Baron visited his brother. He had a great shock when he heard about his son's wedding. And at once he thought of another wicked plan.

"Let us go for a walk, my dear, and get to know each other," he said to her. "We'll go around the city walls if you like." She agreed willingly but when they had climbed to the highest part, the Baron seized her round the waist and was going to throw her over the wall.

The girl begged him to spare her life. "I've never done anything to you," she cried, "why do you hate me and want to kill me?"

"I did not want you to marry my son," he said coldly. "I cannot forgive you for doing this."

"Please do not kill me," the girl sobbed. "I will leave this city at once and I promise that I will never try to see you or your son again unless you ask me to come back."

The Baron thought for a moment then he let go of her. He took a heavy gold ring off his finger and threw it over the wall into the rushing river far below where it disappeared under the water. "Go then," he shouted at the frightened girl. "Never dare to show your face again until you can show me that ring." He laughed cruelly and marched away.

The poor girl kept her promise and slipped away quietly from the city. She wandered about for days until she came to a wonderful castle. She crept to the kitchens and begged the cook to give her some work. The cook took pity on her and the girl was allowed to stay and she worked hard for her keep.

One day many visitors arrived at the castle and who should walk into the great hall but the Baron, his brother and his son! The girl was terrified for she knew her life would be in danger if the Baron saw her. "I'll be safe if I stay in the kitchen," she thought, "he will not look for me here, though I should like to see my husband once again." She sighed as she went on with her work.

The cook asked her to clean and cook an enormous fish. As she was doing this her fingers touched something hard and she pulled out a beautiful gold ring. It was the same ring which the Baron had thrown into the river.

"The fish must have swallowed this ring!" the girl exclaimed. "Who would have believed I should see it again!" She washed and dried it and slipped it into her pocket. She arranged the fish very nicely on a silver dish, which a servant carried to the hall.

The guests soon tasted the fish. "Excellent!" one shouted, and everybody agreed.

"Who cooked this fish?" demanded the Baron.

"I don't know," said the owner of the castle, "but I will find out." He called a servant to his side: "Go to the kitchen, find the cook of this excellent fish and send her here at once."

Everybody stared in surprise when they saw such a beautiful cook enter the room. The Baron jumped to his feet.

"You!" he shouted, "You know what I promised to do if you ever came near me or my son!" and he pulled out a dagger. The girl was unafraid and walked calmly towards him. She pulled the ring out of her pocket and placed it on the table. "I ask you to remember *your* promise, Baron," she said quietly. The Baron stared, speechless. Then he took her hand. "Three times I've tried to get rid of you and three times I have failed. I should have believed what the Book of Magic told me. I know now that you are my son's true wife." He led her to the seat next to his son and later they went back to the Baron's castle where they lived very happily together from that day on.

THE PATCHWORK QUILT

Far in the north, where the snow falls for three hundred days each year, and all the trees are Christmas trees, there was an old lady making patchwork. Her name was Mrs Noot. She had many, many little three-cornered pieces of cloth – boxes full and baskets full, bags full and bundles full, all the colours of the rainbow. There were red pieces and blue pieces, pink pieces and golden pieces. Some had flowers on, some were plain.

Mrs Noot sewed twelve pieces into a star. Then she sewed the stars together to make bigger stars. And then she sewed *those* together. She sewed them with gold thread and silver thread and white thread and black thread.

What do you suppose she was making?

She was making a quilt for the bed of her little grandson Nils. She had nearly finished. When she had put in the last star, little Nils would have the biggest and brightest and warmest and most beautiful quilt in the whole of the north country – perhaps in the whole world.

While his granny sewed, little Nils sat beside her and watched the way her needle flashed in and out of the coloured pieces, making little tiny stitches.

Sometimes he said,

"Is it nearly done, Granny?"

He had asked her this question every day for a year. Each time he asked it, Mrs Noot would sing,

"Moon and candle
Give me your light,
Fire in the hearth
Burn clear, burn bright.

Needle fly swiftly,
Thread run fast,
Until the quilt
Is done at last.

The finest quilt
That ever was,
Made from more than
A thousand stars!"

This was a magic song, to help her sew quickly. While she sang it, little Nils would sit silent on his stool, stroking the bright colours of the quilt. And the fire would stop crackling to listen, and the wind would hush its blowing.

Now the quilt was nearly done.

It would be ready in time for Nils' birthday.

Far, far to the south of Mrs Noot's cottage, in the hot, dry country where there is no grass and it rains only once every three years, a wizard lived in the desert. His name was Ali Beg.

Ali Beg was very lazy. All day he slept in the sun, lying on a magic carpet, while twelve camels stood around it, shading him. At night he went flying on his carpet. But even then the unhappy camels were not allowed to sit down. They had to stand in a square, each with a green lamp hanging on a chain round its neck, so that when Ali Beg came home he could see where to land in the dark. The poor camels were tired out, and very hungry too, because they never had enough to eat.

As well as being unkind to his camels, Ali Beg was a thief. Everything he had was stolen – his clothes, his magic carpet, his camels, even the green lights on their necks. (They were really traffic lights; Ali Beg had stolen them from the city of Beirut one day as he flew over, so all the traffic had come to a stop.)

In a box, Ali Beg kept a magic eye which could see all the beautiful things everywhere in the world. Every night he looked into the eye and chose something new to steal.

One day, when Ali Beg was lying fast asleep, the eldest of the camels said, "Friends, I am faint with hunger. I must have something to eat."

The youngest camel said, "As there is no grass, let us eat the carpet."

So they began to nibble the edge of the carpet. It was thick and soft and silky. They nibbled and nibbled, they munched and munched, until there was nothing left but the bit under Ali Beg.

When he woke up he was very angry.

"Wicked camels! I am going to beat you with my umbrella and you shall have no food for a year. Now I have all the trouble of finding another carpet."

When he had beaten the camels, Ali Beg took his magic eye out of its box. He said to it:

> "Find me a carpet
> Magic Eye,
> To carry me far
> And carry me high."

Then he looked into the magic eye to see what he could see. The eye went dark, and then it went bright.

What Ali Beg could see then was the kitchen of Mrs Noot's cottage. There she sat, by her big fireplace, sewing away at the wonderful patchwork quilt.

"Aha!" said Ali Beg. "I can see that it is a magic quilt – just the thing for me."

He jumped on what was left of the magic carpet. He had to sit astride, the way you do on a horse, because there was so little left.

"Carry me, carpet,
Carry me fast,
Through burning sun,
Through wintry blast.

With never a slip
And never a tilt,
Carry me straight
To the magic quilt."

The piece of carpet carried him up into the air. But it was so small it could not go very fast. In fact, it went so slowly that, as it crept along, Ali Beg was burned black by the hot sun. Then, when he came to the cold north country where Mrs Noot lived, he was frozen by the cold.

By now night had fallen. The carpet was going slower and slower and slower – lower and lower and lower. At last it sank down on a mountain top. It was quite worn out. Ali Beg angrily stepped off and walked down the mountain to Mrs Noot's house.

He looked through the window. Little Nils was in bed fast asleep. Tomorrow would be his birthday.

Mrs Noot had sat up late to finish the quilt. There was only one star left to put in. But she had fallen asleep in her chair, with the needle halfway through a patch.

Ali Beg softly lifted the latch.

He tiptoed in.

Very, very gently, so as not to wake Mrs Noot, he pulled the beautiful red and blue and green and crimson and pink and gold quilt from under her hands. He never noticed the needle. Mrs Noot never woke up.

Ali Beg stole out of the door, carrying the quilt.

He spread it out on the snow. Even in the moonlight, its colours showed bright. Ali Beg sat down on it. He said,

> "By hill and dale,
> Over forest and foam
> Carry me safely
> Carry me home!"

Old Mrs Noot had stitched a lot of magic into the quilt as she sewed and sang. It was even better than the carpet. It rose up into the air and carried Ali Beg south towards the hot country.

When Mrs Noot woke and found her beautiful quilt gone, she and little Nils hunted for it everywhere, but it was not in the kitchen – nor in the woodshed – nor in the forest – nowhere.

Although it was his birthday, little Nils cried all day.

Back in the desert, Ali Beg lay down on the quilt and went to sleep. The camels stood round, shading him.

Then the youngest camel said, "Friends, I have been thinking. Why should we keep the sun off this wicked man while he sleeps on a soft quilt? Let us roll him onto the sand and sit on the quilt ourselves. Then we can make it take us away and leave him behind."

Three camels took hold of Ali Beg's clothes with their teeth and pulled him off the quilt. Then they all sat on it in a ring, round the star-shaped hole in the middle. (Luckily it was a *very* big quilt.)

The eldest camel said,

> "Beautiful quilt,
> So fine and grand,
> Carry us home
> To your native land."

At once the quilt rose up in the air, with all the camels sitting on it.

At that moment, Ali Beg woke. He saw them up above him. With a shout of rage, he jumped up and made a grab for the quilt. His fingers just caught in the star-shaped hole.

The quilt sailed along with Ali Beg hanging underneath.

The youngest camel said, "Friends, let us get rid of Ali Beg. He is too heavy for this quilt."

So all the camels humped and bumped and thumped, they knocked and rocked, they slipped and tipped, they wriggled and jiggled, until the needle which Mrs Noot had left sticking through a patch ran into Ali Beg's finger. He gave a yell and let go. He fell down and down, down and down and down, until he hit the sea with a great SPLASH.

And that was the end of Ali Beg.

But the quilt sailed on, with the camels. As they flew over Beirut, they threw down the twelve green traffic lights.

When at last they landed outside Mrs Noot's house, Nils came running out.

"Oh, Granny!" he cried. "Come and see! The quilt has come back! And it has brought me twelve camels for a birthday present."

"Dear me," said Mrs Noot, "I shall have to make them jackets, or they will find it too cold in these parts."

So she made them beautiful patchwork jackets and gave them plenty of hot porridge to eat. The camels were very happy to have found such a kind home.

Mrs Noot sewed the last star into the patchwork and spread the quilt on Nils' bed.

"There," she said. "Now it's bedtime!"

Nils jumped into bed and lay proudly under his beautiful quilt. He went straight to sleep. And what wonderful dreams he had that night, and every night after, while his granny sat in front of the big fire, with six camels on either side of her.

THE TONGUE-CUT SPARROW

Many years ago an old man and his wife lived in a little house in Japan.

The old man worked hard in the woods and fields. He liked working outside for then he need not listen to the grumbles of his wife. Nothing was ever right for her and she always seemed to be cross about something.

Sad to say they hadn't any children but the old man had a tame sparrow which he loved very much. After he had worked hard all day, he would play with his little pet. He usually opened the sparrow's cage. She then flew around the room and sat on his finger. He talked to her and taught her some funny little tricks, and often gave her special things to eat which he'd saved from his supper.

One day the old man was in the fields and the old woman was washing clothes. She liked to starch them but today all the starch she had mixed had gone. The bowl was empty!

"Who could have taken my starch?" she wondered.

The little sparrow in her cage bowed her head in the Japanese way.

"I took your starch," she chirped. "I thought you had put out some food for me so I took it. I didn't know it was your starch. Please forgive me."

The old woman was very angry. She hated the sparrow and did not like her husband to talk or play with it. Secretly she was jealous for she knew her husband loved the little bird very much. Now there was a chance to hurt it. She seized the sparrow and shook her.

"You licked up my starch with your tongue but it won't happen again. I'll make your tongue sorry for this." With these words, she seized her sharp scissors and cut the poor sparrow's tongue. Then she threw the bird outside even though it was chirping in great pain.

At night the old man returned. He took off his straw sandals, for nobody in Japan wears shoes indoors. He looked for his pet. The cage was empty. He peered around the room and all around the veranda, then he called his wife.

"Wife, have you seen my little sparrow today?"

"No I haven't," she lied. "I expect she's flown away to a better home, ungrateful little thing."

The old man looked everywhere but he could not see the sparrow. Then he started asking his wife many questions over and over again.

"All right, I suppose I'd better tell you," the old woman said at last. "The silly thing ate all my starch then she boasted about what she'd done. I cut her tongue to punish her. Then I chased the nasty little bird away."

Her husband was very upset. "How unkind and cruel," he whispered. "You must have given my little pet a lot of pain and she won't be able to sing or chirp properly with a cut tongue. How could you have done this?"

His wife went to bed early as she was cross with her husband for scolding her. He could not sleep but sat in his chair.

"What shall I do?" he asked himself. "I know! Tomorrow I'll go and search the fields and woods," and at last he dozed off.

At dawn next day he had breakfast and set off. In hedgerows and clumps of bamboos he called gently:

"Where oh where is my tongue-cut sparrow?"

He went further and further and did not stop to eat. Then as the sun was setting he stopped at the edge of a bamboo grove to rest. "I'll call for the last time," he thought, "then I must go home: sweet sparrow, please answer me."

His voice was low and sad but this time he could hear a little chirp, chirp! There was a small sparrow on a branch. He ran forward and the bird started to do all the tricks he had taught her. Then she perched on his fingers.

"It is you, my poor little tongue-cut sparrow," he cried with joy. "I am very sorry about your tongue and my unkind wife. But at least I've found you. I'm so happy now."

"Do not worry any more," chirped the sparrow. "See, my tongue was sewn up by a wise old owl. It does not hurt and it is

quite better now."

"That is good news. I shall call you Lady Sparrow from now on," the old man said, "for I can see you are no ordinary bird."

The Lady Sparrow led him into the middle of the bamboo trees and there he saw a beautiful house. It was made from white wood and when he had taken off his sandals, he went inside. There he saw that the floors were covered with the finest cream-coloured carpets. All the cushions were made from softest silk. In special cupboards, or tokonoma as they are called in Japan, there were vases, jewels and lacquered boxes.

The old man was led to the best cushion and then the Lady Sparrow bowed to him many times. At each bow, she thanked him for taking care of her so well in his house. Then she clapped her hands and all her daughters came fluttering in. They carried many dishes and soon a wonderful feast was spread out in front of him. While he was eating they danced the Suzume-odori which is

33

the Japanese name for the Sparrow's Dance.

The old man laughed and clapped his hands. Then he noticed that it was very dark outside.

"I must leave you," he told the Lady Sparrow. "I have a long way to go. I am very late already and my wife will be cross because she expects me to get home every day at exactly the same time."

"Please stay and rest a little longer," the sparrows begged him. "Do not hurry away."

But he shook his head. "I'll visit you whenever I can, now that I know where your house is. But I must go now."

The Lady Sparrow asked her daughters to bring in two wicker baskets. They put them down in front of the old man; one was heavy and one was light.

"Now choose one of these baskets to take home as a present," he was told.

"I think I'll take the lighter one," he said. "The other is too heavy for me to carry a long way." Also, he did not think it was

polite to choose the bigger basket.

The sparrow helped to tie the basket to his back then they all bowed low. "Please be sure to come back again," they called as he set off through the bamboos.

When he reached home his wife was waiting in the doorway. "Where have you been?" she demanded crossly. "Don't you know what time it is?"

He told her about the bamboo wood and where he had found the sparrow and her wonderful house. He showed her the wicker basket. "Shall we look at my basket?" he said. "You can help me to open it if you like."

What a surprise they had. The basket was filled to the top with gold and silver coins and precious jewels.

"Now that we have all this money, I won't have to work hard all day in the fields," the old man said. "And you can have nice clothes and good food, my dear, from now on. And for all this we must thank my little sparrow."

They poured the wonderful gifts back into the basket. The old man kept saying "Thank you, my little sparrow, thank you, my little sparrow," over and over again.

"There is enough for us here for the rest of our lives," he chuckled. "I'm very glad I didn't choose the heavier basket."

"Heavier basket! What do you mean? Was there a bigger one?" his wife demanded. He nodded.

"You stupid old fellow," screamed the wife. "Think of all the gold and silver we have lost, twice as much as this I expect. What a fool you are."

She was greedy as well as bad-tempered! At once she forgot how cruel she had been to the sparrow. She wanted to get more money and jewels. So she planned to find the sparrow and get the heavier basket.

Next day, she set off at dawn and at last she found the bamboo grove that her husband had described to her. She rushed towards the sparrow's house and banged loudly on the door. Some little servant-birds told the Lady Sparrow that her old and cruel mistress was outside and wanted to visit her. She was surprised for she had never expected to see her again. But she went out and greeted her visitor politely.

"I won't waste any time," the old woman said roughly. "You and your daughters needn't get any food ready for me. Just tell your servants to bring me the other basket, the heavy one. My husband was so stupid to leave it behind. That's all I've come for. So hurry up then and I'll be on my way."

The Lady Sparrow was even more surprised at these rude words, but she ordered her servants to bring out the heavy basket. The old woman grabbed it and put it on her back. She didn't mutter a single word of thanks or give the smallest bow, but turned around and rushed towards home.

She longed to open the basket for she wanted to see how much gold there was inside and at last she stopped and greedily flung open the basket. But instead of gold and silver, horrible little monsters were sitting there. They jumped and danced around. They screamed and they screeched. They pulled ugly faces and put out their tongues. The old woman had never been so scared in all her life. She jumped up and ran and ran all the way home.

She threw herself inside the cottage and bolted the door. Then she burst into tears and told her husband what had happened. "Your friend the sparrow did this to me," she wailed. "I only wanted the heavy basket which you should have taken. She is a nasty little bird. How can you be her friend?"

But her husband held up his hand and stopped her.

"You were very unkind to the sparrow and cut her tongue. And you were rude and very greedy. I hope you will never behave like this again."

Those horrible creatures had given her such a scare that she didn't say another word. She went to bed and the next day she forgot to grumble once. To everybody's surprise she stopped grumbling altogether. She became gentle and polite and she and her husband lived happily for many years, using the treasure which had come from the tongue-cut sparrow.

THE EMPEROR'S NEW CLOTHES

There was once an Emperor who was very vain. He loved to wear expensive clothes and tried to look as splendid as possible all the time. In his palace he had many rooms full of wardrobes and chests of fine clothes, and he liked to admire himself in long mirrors every time he changed, which he did several times a day. Cloth merchants and tailors grew rich by supplying clothes to the Emperor, and many beautifully coloured and finely-woven materials were imported from faraway lands for the Emperor to choose from. Many people used to laugh at him for his vanity, but he was too proud to notice.

One day two swindlers, pretending to be cloth merchants, came to the Emperor's palace and asked to see the Emperor. They told the servants they had come from a faraway land with cloth more beautiful than anything the Emperor had ever seen before. When the palace servants asked to see the cloth, they were told it was for the Emperor's eyes alone.

The Emperor was so excited when he heard about the visitors that he arranged to see them immediately. They bowed low before him, and said that they had come to offer him the finest material in the whole world. It was so fine, they told him, that it had the magical quality of being invisible to anyone who was a fool. The Emperor asked to see it at once, so the two scoundrels opened their big wooden trunk and pretended to take out first one roll of cloth and then another. The Emperor blinked for he could see no cloth at all, even though the men did look as if they were unrolling some.

"I cannot let them think I am a fool," he thought to himself, so he pretended he could see the material perfectly well.

"Look at the lovely colours!" said one scoundrel.

"And the fine gold thread!" said the other, as they held up the invisible cloth before the Emperor.

"Yes," said the Emperor, sounding as enthusiastic as he could. "The colours are beautiful and the design magnificent."

He called in his wife and the Chief Minister and some of the courtiers to admire the cloth, and he explained about its magic qualities. They too could see no cloth at all, but they did not want the Emperor to think they were fools, so one by one they all admired the cloth. The Emperor was slightly disappointed because he had always thought that his wife and the Chief Minister were very foolish. But when they admired the material and talked about it, even putting out their hands to touch it, he decided he must have been wrong about them all the time. If they could see it, he certainly wasn't going to announce that he could not.

"Would your Majesty like us to take your measurements so that a suit can be made for you from these fine materials?" the merchants asked. "We will make it up ourselves, for we can trust nobody else to cut it and stitch it."

The Emperor agreed to have a suit made and promised to reward the merchants well with money and jewels.

The scoundrels were given a room in the palace for their work. One material was chosen for the jacket, another for the trousers. A special shirt with lace collar and cuffs was also to be made from the material in the merchants' chest. The Emperor was very particular about where he wanted the buttons and how tight the waist was to be, and the scoundrels fussed around him, making careful notes of all his wishes.

The next day the Emperor went to try on his new clothes. He took off all his clothes and allowed the merchants to dress him, although he could not see what they were putting on. Then he walked across to the long mirror. He turned round and round but he could see no clothes at all. He called his Chief Minister who was astonished to see the Emperor standing before him with no clothes on, but not wishing to appear a fool, he said,

"How magnificent Your Majesty looks. How splendid! Why not wear this wonderful suit of new clothes at your birthday procession next week?"

"The Chief Minister is not such a fool after all!" thought the Emperor, and agreed that he would wear the clothes when he rode through the city at the head of the great procession.

Around the city the news spread that the Emperor would be wearing the finest clothes ever seen on his birthday, and the crowds gathered in the streets to see him. Everyone had also heard that only wise people would see the new clothes as, to fools, they would be invisible, and everyone had secretly decided that

they would rather pretend to see them than let their friends and neighbours think they were fools.

The Emperor dressed with care on the day, flicking specks of dust off the wonderful new clothes he could not see, and admiring himself in the mirror for even longer than usual until the Master of Ceremonies came to say that the crowds were growing impatient. It was time for the procession to begin.

As he rode through the streets the Emperor heard the crowds cheering, and thought, "How lucky I am to rule over so many wise people. It seems there are no fools in my country, for everyone can see my new clothes."

But there was one small boy who had climbed a tree to get a better view of the Emperor. He had not heard that the Emperor's clothes were only visible to wise people, and he shouted out at once, "What has happened to his clothes? The Emperor hasn't anything on at all!"

The crowd laughed uneasily, then someone else shouted out, "The boy is right! The Emperor has got no clothes on!"

The laughter of the crowds turned on the Emperor and then on themselves, for they realized they had all been fools to believe the story of the magic clothes.

The Emperor was very angry with the scoundrels who had tricked him, and sent for them as soon as he got back to the palace. But they had fled, taking with them all the money and jewels the Emperor had given them. And you may be sure they were never seen in that country again.

Then the Emperor sent for the little boy who had climbed the tree and called out that he could not see the clothes. He told the boy he was the only wise person in the whole country, for he was not afraid to speak the truth. The Emperor promised him that he would be the Chief Minister when he grew up.

ALI BABA
AND THE FORTY THIEVES

Long ago in a warm and sunny land there were two brothers. Kassim, the older brother, married a very rich but bad-tempered wife and with her money he bought a busy shop in the market. Kassim and his wife were very greedy and would not help anyone, even when they were in great trouble. Nobody liked them – except Ali Baba the younger brother who loved everybody.

Now Ali Baba was very poor. He was a woodcutter and his wife was cheerful and kind-hearted but she had no money either. They lived together with their son and daughter, and would have been very happy if they had not been so poor.

One day Ali Baba and his three donkeys went up into the forest as usual. He started to cut wood near some enormous rocks at the edge of the mountains. His donkeys nibbled the grass while he worked. It was quiet except for the noise of his axe against the tree trunks. He stopped for a rest and he heard another noise. It was the sound of many galloping horses and at once he was scared because he knew that robbers lived in the mountains. Very quickly he hid his axe, then he led his donkeys into the forest and tied them under some bushes.

"Don't bray or move," he begged them, then he climbed into a tree to watch what was happening.

Almost at once, the galloping noise of horses grew louder and Ali Baba saw a band of fierce horsemen appearing around the rocks. They had thick black beards; some had daggers in their mouths and all of them carried curved swords.

"One, two, three . . ." Ali Baba counted to himself. "Thirty-nine altogether and that one must be the captain."

He shivered for the captain looked even more fierce and wicked than the other thirty-nine men.

They got down from their horses, and unloaded the bags which had been fastened to their saddles. Next, they tied the horses so that they could not run away. Then they carried the heavy bags one by one to the foot of the biggest rock which had smooth sides as tall as a house. When they were all piled up neatly and the robbers were standing in a line, the captain shouted in a terrible voice, "Open Sesame!"

There was a noise like a clap of thunder and the rock opened just a little. Then with a roar it opened a little more and when the crack was wide enough, each robber in turn picked up his saddle-bag and disappeared inside. The robber-captain went in last of all. "Shut Sesame!" he yelled and the crack shut tight with a grinding noise.

"I pray they don't find me in this tree," muttered Ali Baba. "They'll kill me if they think I know their secret." He looked anxiously towards the bushes where his donkeys were hidden. "Please don't move, little donkeys. I'll give you extra food later but stay hidden now, I beg you."

Ali Baba was frightened to move in case the robbers appeared again so he stayed in the tree. Then he heard loud noises. The rock

split open. All the robbers marched out in line and each one carried an empty saddle bag this time. They untied their horses and fastened on the bags again. They mounted their horses and then waited. Ali Baba counted thirty-nine. At last the robber-chief came out as well. He shouted "Shut Sesame!" and watched until the rock shut tightly again. He leapt on his horse, waved his sword and the whole gang of robbers galloped away, shouting loudly as they went.

Ali Baba waited, still trembling with fear, until he was sure that the robbers had gone. When it was quiet again he climbed down from the tree and rushed over to his donkeys.

"You are good little donkeys," he said as he untied them. "You did not make even a little noise." He took them back to the edge of the rock where they nibbled the grass once more.

Ali Baba went over to the special rock with the smooth side. He was quite curious and he wondered how a rock could open so easily. He looked at it closely and carefully. He rubbed his hands

all over it as far as he could reach but the rock was clean and smooth.

"There isn't a crack anywhere," he said. "I can't even find a place where I could push a needle in."

He was very puzzled so he sat down on the grass to think.

"There must be some magic here," he decided. "Now, I must think carefully and remember exactly what those robbers and their chief did. First of all, they piled up the bags then that horrible-looking chief stood in front and I'm sure I heard him say 'sesame'. But my wife buys sesame seeds in the market to use when she is baking! That can't be right." He got up and stood in front of the rock again. "Yet I only heard those two words. I wonder if they are the magic ones? Well, I can try them can't I?"

He was talking to make himself feel a little bit braver and as he moved closer to the rock he whispered in a very shaky voice "Open Sesame".

At once the rock obeyed his order. With a roar like thunder, a crack appeared in the smooth rock. This soon grew wide enough for a man to walk through. Ali Baba looked up carefully, for he'd thrown himself face down on the grass when he heard the thundering noise. At first he was too frightened to move. "Get up," he told himself. "You can be as brave as those robbers, can't you?" and he got up to his feet. He tiptoed across to the rock. He plucked up all his courage and peeped inside.

To his amazement he saw a long passage and this led into an enormous cave. All this had been dug out of the inside of the mountain. There were even slits cut into the roof to let a little sunlight in.

Ali Baba stepped inside but he was terrified in case the robber gang came back and spotted him. Then he remembered the captain's other words! So he called "Shut Sesame" and at once the crack in the rock closed behind him.

He felt much braver now and thought he might as well explore and see for himself what the robbers had carried into the cave. He walked carefully along and soon he reached the huge cave at the end of the passage.

He looked around and saw many shelves which went right up to the roof. Every one of them was filled up with treasure. There were bars of silver and gold, bags of money and rolls and rolls of silks and satins. On the floor there were chests all filled with diamonds, rubies, pearls and more gold coins. These chests were so full that many treasures had fallen onto the ground. Ali Baba almost tripped up and he saw that he had walked into a pile of crowns covered with jewels.

"Those thieves must have been busy for a long time for there is so much treasure here. And now I will be able to use some of it for my family. We won't be poor any longer."

This made Ali Baba feel so happy and he remembered his three donkeys and the extra feed he had promised them.

"I wonder how many things my donkeys can carry? I must work this out. Oh, but first I must decide what to take. Shall I choose emeralds or diamonds or these crowns?" Ali Baba was talking aloud as he made his plans. "If I take any of those things then all the people in the market will wonder where I found them. They might think I was a thief! No, I'll take gold coins for they are easy to pack and easy to sell, and the robbers won't notice that I've taken them."

He spotted six bags and he filled them with gold coins. He carried the bags one by one as they were quite heavy, to the end of the passage. Then he said "Open Sesame," and the rock opened in front of him. His donkeys were just outside so he fastened two bags on the back of each one. He remembered to turn around and say "Shut Sesame" for he did not want the robbers' captain to know that someone had discovered his secret. He spread a few light pieces of wood over the donkeys so that the bags were hidden and he picked up his axe from its hiding place as well.

They had to walk quite slowly from the forest to the city because the gold was heavy and Ali Baba was a kind man who did not want to make his donkeys work too hard. It was night time when they got back and Ali Baba's wife was waiting in the little courtyard outside their house. As soon as the donkeys could not be seen by any passers-by, Ali Baba pulled the pieces of wood off their backs and his wife noticed the six bags.

"What are these, my husband?" asked the wife. "They do not belong to us. Where did you get them?"

"They are a special present, good wife. Please help me to carry them and I'll answer your questions later."

"How heavy they are," the wife thought. She heard the clink, clink of money as she staggered into the house with one bag, and the poor woman was very frightened. Where had the coins come from? Why was her husband so late home?

"They may bring bad luck. Don't open them. Take them all away again," she begged.

Ali Baba locked the door and closed the shutters on the windows. "Don't say another word, wife, until you've seen what I've brought." Then he poured golden coins on the floor in front of her.

She was then even more frightened, so Ali Baba told her all that had happened that day and about his amazing discoveries in the mountainside.

Then his wife was overjoyed and she was very proud of her husband for bringing so much gold safely back. They and their children were able to live even better than Kassim and his wife for many years to come.

CAP O'RUSHES

Long ago a rich man lived in a beautiful home. He had three daughters and they were all very happy together. But then one day he thought he would like to find out which of his daughters loved him the most. He asked them to come to him in the sitting-room and he said to the eldest:

"How much do you love me, dearest daughter?"

"As much as I love my own life, dear father," she replied.

"That is good," said the father. He looked at his second daughter.

"How much do you love me, dearest daughter?"

"Better than anything you can find in the whole world, dear father," she said.

"That is very good." The father looked very pleased as he turned to his youngest daughter and asked the same question.

"How much do you love me, dearest daughter?"

"I love you as much as meat needs salt," she said with a sweet smile.

"What!" exclaimed the father. "That is not a proper answer to my question, it shows that you do not love me, even a little. You ungrateful girl, get out of my sight and do not return here ever again."

He was so angry that he made her leave the house at once. The poor girl was very sad because she loved her father very much. She wandered over the fields and through dark woods then she sat on the banks of a little stream to have a rest. She saw many tall green rushes growing at the edge of the water and she had an idea.

"If I pick a big bunch of rushes, I can weave them in and out. Then I can make a cloak and hood for myself. These will cover me up." She knew that nobody would believe that she hadn't any money if they saw her fine gown.

Through the trees she saw a grand house so she walked

around until she came to the back door. She knocked timidly and the cook came to the door.

"Have you any work for me?" she asked.

"There's no job here unless you can clean pots and pans," the cook told her. "It's hard work – you don't look strong enough to me."

"Oh there's no job that I, Cap o' Rushes, can't do," the girl said quickly.

"Come in then, Cap o' Rushes, if that's your name. You can start scouring that lot of pans."

The master of the house loved giving parties and a few days later he invited many friends to a feast with dancing afterwards. The cook was very busy getting the food ready while Cap o' Rushes cleared and scoured hundreds of dishes all day long.

When the kitchen was clean and tidy, the other servants went to watch the dancing in the ballroom. All except Cap o' Rushes! She hurried to the servants' rooms and took off her cloak and hood. She put on a beautiful silver gown, then she slipped along a quiet passage until she came to the ballroom. She walked inside but she didn't watch the dancing like the other servants. Instead

she joined the guests and soon all the young men were begging her to dance.

Everyone wondered who the mysterious girl was.

"She is the loveliest girl I've ever seen," the son of the master of the house thought. They danced every dance and he fell in love with her. Cap o' Rushes knew she must not stay until the end so she slipped away quietly.

Next day, all the servants were talking about the party and the beautiful girl in the silver dress. Cap o' Rushes picked up some pots and pans and turned away. She didn't say a word but she smiled secretly.

For days and days the master's son tried to find the girl he'd fallen in love with. He asked all his friends if they knew her, but they could not tell him anything.

Soon, the master of the house gave another party and again the servants were allowed to watch the dancing.

"Come with us," the cook told Cap o' Rushes.

"I had so many pots and pans to clean today, I'm very tired," replied the girl. So the servants went without her.

At once Cap o' Rushes went to change. She took off her cloak and this time she wore a beautiful gold dress.

The master's son was waiting anxiously by the door and he was so happy when she came in. He took her hand and danced all evening with her. But before the end of the party Cap o' Rushes made another excuse to leave early. Her gown was put away and she was fast asleep when the others came to bed.

"I wish you didn't get so tired because you missed another lovely party," the cook told her the next morning. "That beautiful girl came again in a shining gold dress this time. The young master could not take his eyes off her. Oh, it was a lovely sight."

"I wish I could have been there." Cap o' Rushes smiled at the kind cook. "Perhaps next time I'll go."

For days the young master searched everywhere trying to find out where his beautiful partner lived. But he was unlucky. Nobody knew anything about her. So he asked his father to have another ball. That would be the third one! His kind father asked all his friends to come again and the servants asked Cap o' Rushes to watch the dancing with them.

"I'm too tired," she declared. As soon as they were out of sight, she took off her cloak and she put on the finest gown of all, in purest white with silver stars.

Of course the master's handsome son was overjoyed to see her. He took her hand and this time he asked her many questions. But she did not give him a single answer. "I think I'll die if I don't see you again," he said sadly. "Please wear my ring whatever happens."

Once again Cap o' Rushes left early and slipped back to bed. She was fast asleep when the others came back. The next morning everybody talked about the girl in white.

The young man searched again for the girl, but nobody could help him. He was so sad that he could not eat and he became thin and weak.

The cook thought she would make some special porridge for him and while she was doing this, Cap o' Rushes walked in.

"Who is that porridge for?" she asked.

"It's for the young master. He is so ill because he loves that girl."

"Let me put it into this special bowl," said Cap o' Rushes. As she did this, she slipped into it the ring the young master had given her.

A footman carried the porridge upstairs. When the young man had finished eating it he saw the ring at the bottom of the bowl. He asked to see the cook immediately.

"Who made this porridge?" he demanded.

"I did, young master, and Cap o' Rushes helped me by pouring the porridge into the bowl."

"Send *her* to me then at once," and the young man dared to smile.

Cap o' Rushes came immediately.

"Did you pour the porridge into this bowl?" he asked.

"Yes," she said quietly.

"Where did you get this ring?" He held it up . . .

"From the one who gave it to me," she said.

"Please tell me who you are!" begged the young master.

She threw back her cloak and underneath she was wearing a shining silver dress.

The young man was overjoyed and soon he felt well and strong again. They planned their wedding day and Cap o' Rushes' father was invited as well as hundreds of other guests.

Cap o' Rushes went to the cook who was getting the wedding feast ready and she said, "Please do not put any salt in the meat. Not even one tiny grain."

"But the meat will be tasteless!" the cook said unhappily.

"It doesn't matter just this once," Cap o' Rushes said. "I have a special reason for this."

Everyone sat down in the hall to enjoy the wedding feast. But after the first bite, nobody ate the meat. It was so tasteless. Then one of the guests sighed deeply.

"Is there something wrong?" the bridegroom asked.

"I asked my daughter once how much she loved me," he replied. " 'As much as fresh meat needs salt', she said. I sent her away but now I know that she loved me very much, and I'll never see her again." He wept sorrowfully.

Cap o' Rushes lifted up her bridal veil. "Look, father, here I am," she cried. She hugged him and everyone cheered at the happy ending of this wedding day.

PANDORA'S BOX

In the country of Greece long ago, people living there were always happy. There was nothing to hurt them so children never cried. Their houses were made from leaves and grasses for the winds blew gently and the sun was always shining.

Epimetheus and his beautiful wife, Pandora, lived in this land. They loved each other very much and stayed together all day long. One day the god Mercury came to visit them. He looked hot and tired for he was carrying a heavy wooden box.

"What is in your box?" Epimetheus asked.

"I cannot tell you that," Mercury answered. "I have a long way to go and this box slows me down. May I leave it in your house for a time? I will collect it on my way back."

"Of course," was the reply. "We will look after it."

"I must give you this warning," Mercury said. "No matter what happens, do not open the box or you will be sorry and unhappy for ever."

"Don't worry, that will not happen. Your box will be safe with us." Epimetheus put it carefully in a corner of their house and Mercury went on his way.

Pandora wondered what was in the box and one day she went quietly into the house while Epimetheus was outside. She looked at the box and then, to her surprise, she heard tiny noises and whispers coming from it. She ran over and knelt down but she could not understand any of the sounds. She touched the golden rope which was tied tightly round the box. She wanted to untie the knot if she could, but just then her husband walked in. "Please come and join the dance my love," he begged.

"I'd rather find out what is in here," Pandora said. "Do you think I could take a little peep?"

"Oh no," Epimetheus was worried. "Mercury said it would make us unhappy. Come outside into the sunshine." But Pandora refused. "I'll come later my dear," she said.

He was very surprised at Pandora's reply as they always stayed together, but he thought she would run outside when she heard the music. So he left her.

Pandora looked at the whispering box. "I'll just undo that gold rope a little," she said softly. She pulled and she struggled but the knot was so tight that it was hard work to make it loose.

"Pandora, come and dance with us in the sunshine," her friends now called to her. But she did not answer. She pulled again and again at the rope until suddenly it was undone! The rope fell on the ground and she could open the box.

"I'll open the lid a tiny bit and take a quick peep. Then I'll close it. That can't hurt me, I'm sure." Pandora thought.

She put her ear close to the lid. The tiny voices were clear and now she understood what they were saying.

"Let us out," she heard. "Beautiful Pandora, we are shut up in the dark. It's like a prison. Please let us out!"

Pandora was surprised. She heard her husband coming. She knew that he would tie up the box very tightly then she would never know what was inside. So quickly she opened the box.

As soon as Pandora lifted the lid, thousands of tiny insects flew out. They flew to Pandora and stung her. Then they swarmed over Epimetheus and stung him. It was the first time they had felt any pain. The insects flew outside and there they stung all the happy people who shouted with pain as well. Epimetheus and Pandora had their first quarrel after she slammed down the lid.

"Look what you have done," he shouted. "Those insects have brought pain and evil things and you are to blame."

Pandora started to cry. Then they heard a small sweet voice calling from the box.

"Let me out! Let me out! I can make you happy again!"

"Shall I open the box?" asked Pandora fearfully.

"You can't make things any worse," her husband said.

This time a pretty white fairy appeared when the lid was opened. "My name is Hope," she told them. "I can't stop you from getting hurt but I can help to make you feel better."

The old stories say that from that day on, pain and trouble came into the world but that we would always have hope. And all because Pandora opened that box!

TIM RABBIT
AND THE SCISSORS

One day Tim Rabbit found a pair of scissors lying on the common. They had been dropped by somebody's mother, when she sat darning somebody's socks. Tim saw them shining in the grass, so he crept up very softly, just in case they might spring at him. Nearer and nearer he crept, but the scissors did not move, so he touched them with his whiskers, very gently, just in case they might bite him. He took a sniff at them, but nothing happened. Then he licked them, boldly, and, as the scissors were closed, he wasn't hurt. He admired the bright glitter of the steel, so he picked them up and carried them carefully home.

"Oh!" cried Mrs Rabbit, when he dragged them into the kitchen. "Oh! Whatever's that shiny thing? A snake? Put it down, Tim!"

"It's a something I've found in the grass!" said Tim, proudly. "It's quite tame."

Mrs Rabbit examined the scissors, twisting and turning them, until she found that they opened and shut. She wisely put them on the table.

"We'll wait till your father comes home," said she. "He's gone to a meeting about the lateness of the swallows this year, but he said he wouldn't be long."

"What have we here?" exclaimed Mr Rabbit when he returned.

"It's something Tim found," said Mrs Rabbit, looking proudly at her son, and Tim held up his head and put his paws behind his back, just as his father did at a public meeting. Mr Rabbit opened the scissors and felt the sharp edges.

"Why! They're shears!" he cried, excitedly. "They will trim the cowslip banks and cut the hay ready for the haystacks, when we gather our provender in the autumn."

"Wait a minute!" he continued, snipping and snapping in the air. "Wait a minute. I'll show you." He ran out, carrying the scissors under his arm. In a few moments he came back with a neat bundle of grass, tied in a little sheaf.

"We can eat this in the peace and safety of our own house, by our own fireside, instead of sitting in the cold open fields," said he. "This is a wonderful thing you have found, Tim."

Tim smiled happily, and asked, "Will it cut other things, Father?"

"Yes, anything you like. Lettuces, lavender, dandelions, daisies, butter, and buttercups," answered Mr Rabbit, but he put the scissors safely out of reach on a high shelf before he had his supper.

The next day, when his parents had gone to visit a neighbour, young Tim climbed on a stool and lifted down the bright scissors. Then he began to cut 'anything'. First he snipped his little sheep's-wool blanket into bits, and then he snapped the leafy tablecloth into shreds. Next he cut into strips the blue window curtains which his mother had embroidered with gossamer threads, and then he spoilt the tiny roller-towel which hung behind the door. He turned his attention on himself, and trimmed

his whiskers till nothing was left. Finally he started to cut off his fur. How delightful it was to see it drop in a flood of soft brown on the kitchen floor! How silky it was! He didn't know he had so much, and he clipped and clipped, twisting his neck and screwing round to the back, till the floor was covered with a furry fleece.

He felt so free and gay, so cool and happy, that he put the scissors away and danced lightly out of the room and on to the common like a dandelion-clock or a thistledown.

Mrs Rabbit met him as she returned with her basket full of lettuces and little cabbage-plants, given to her by the kind neighbour, who had a garden near the village. She nearly fainted when she saw the strange white dancing little figure.

"Oh! Oh! Oh!" she shrieked. "Whatever's this?"

"Mother, it's me," laughed Tim, leaping round her like a newly-shorn lamb.

"No, it's not my Tim," she cried sadly. "My Tim is a fat fluffy little rabbit. You are a white rat, escaped from a menagerie. Go away."

"Mother, it *is* me!" persisted Tim. "It's Tim, your own Timothy Rabbit." He danced and leaped over the basket which Mrs Rabbit had dropped on the ground.

"No! No! Go away!" she exclaimed, running into her house and shutting the door.

Tim flopped on the doorstep. One big tear rolled down his cheek and splashed on the grass. Then another and another followed in a stream.

"It *is* me," he sobbed, with his nose against the crack of the door.

Inside the house Mrs Rabbit was gathering up the fur.

"It must have been Tim after all," she sighed. "This is his pretty hair. Oh, deary, deary me! Whatever shall I do?"

She opened the door. Tim popped his nose inside and sneezed.

"A-tishoo! A-tishoo! I'm so cold. A-tishoo! I won't do it again. I will be good," he sniffed.

"Come in, young rabbit," said Mrs Rabbit, severely. "Get into bed at once, while I make a dose of hot camomile tea."

But when Tim crept into bed there was no blanket. Poor Mrs Rabbit covered him with her own patchwork quilt, and then gave him the hot posset.

"Now you must stay here till your fur grows again," said Mrs Rabbit, and Tim lay underneath the red and blue patches of the bed-cover, thinking of the fun on the common, the leaping and galloping and turning somersaults of the little rabbits of the burrows, and he would not be there to join in.

Mr Rabbit was thoroughly shocked when he came home and saw his son, but he was a rabbit of ingenuity. He went out at once to borrow a spinning-wheel from an ancient rabbit who made coats to wrap Baby-Buntings in.

All day Mrs Rabbit wove the bits of fur, to make a little brown coat to keep Tim warm. When all the hairs were used up she pinned it round Tim with a couple of tiny sharp thorns from her pin-cushion.

"There you are, dressed again in your own fur," said she, and she put a stitch here and there to make it fit.

How all the animals laughed when Tim ran out on the common, with his little white legs peeping out from the bottom of the funny short coat! How ashamed he was of his whiskerless face!

"Baa! Baa! White sheep! Have you any wool?" mocked his enemies the magpies, when he ran near the wall where they perched. But Tim's fur soon grew again, and then his troubles were over.

He hung his little coat on a gorse-bush for the chaffinches to take for their nest, and very glad they were to get it, too. As for the scissors, they are still lying on the high shelf, and you may see them if you peep down the rabbit hole on the edge of the common where Tim Rabbit lives.

THE FISHERMAN'S SON

A long time ago, when impossible things were possible, there was a fisherman and his son. One day when the fisherman hauled in his net he found a huge gleaming red fish amongst the rest of his catch. For a few moments he was so excited he could only stare at it. "This fish will make me famous," he thought. "Never before has a fisherman caught such a fish."

"Stay here," he said to his son, "and look after these fish, while I go and fetch the cart to take them home."

The fisherman's son, too, was excited by the great red fish, and while he was waiting for his father, he stroked it and started to talk to it.

"It seems a shame that a beautiful creature like you should not swim free," he said, and no sooner had he spoken than he decided to put the fish back into the sea. The great red fish slipped gratefully into the water, raised its head and spoke to the boy.

"It was kind of you to save my life. Take this bone which I have pulled from my fin. If ever you need my help, hold it up, call me, and I will come at once."

The fisherman's son placed the bone carefully in his pocket just as his father reappeared with the cart. When the father saw that his son had let the great red fish go he was angry beyond belief.

"Get out of my sight," he shouted at his son, "and never let me set eyes on you again."

The boy went off sadly. He did not know where to go or what to do.

In time he found himself in a great forest. He walked on and on, till suddenly he was startled by a stag rushing through the trees towards him. It was being chased by a pack of ferocious hounds followed by hunters, and it was clearly exhausted and could run no further.

The boy felt sorry for the stag and took hold of its antlers as the hounds and then the hunters appeared.

"Shame on you," he said, "for chasing a tame stag. Go and find a wild beast to hunt for your sport."

The hunters, seeing the stag standing quietly by the boy thought it must be a pet and so they turned and rode off to another part of the forest.

"It was most kind of you to save my life," said the stag, and it pulled a fine brown hair from its coat. "Take this and if ever you need help, hold it out and call me. I will come at once."

The fisherman's son put the hair in his pocket with the fishbone. He thanked the stag which disappeared among the trees and wandered on once more.

As he walked he heard a strange fluttering sound overhead and, looking up, he saw a great bird – a crane – being attacked by an eagle. The crane was weak and could fight no more, and the eagle was about to kill it. The kindhearted boy picked up a stick

and threw it at the eagle, which flew off at once, fearful of this new enemy. The crane sank to the ground.

"It was kind of you to save my life," it said as it recovered its breath. "Take this feather and keep it safe. If ever you need help, hold it up and call me, and I will come."

As the fisherman's son walked on with the feather in his pocket, he met a fox running for its life, with the hounds and the huntsmen close behind. The boy just had time to hide the fox under his coat before the hounds were all around him.

"I think the fox went that way," he cried to the huntsmen, and they called off the hounds and went in the direction the boy was pointing.

"Thank you for saving my life," said the fox. "Take this hair from my coat and keep it safe. If you ever need my help, hold out the hair and call me. I will come at once."

The fisherman's son went on his way, and in time he reached the edge of the forest and found himself by a lovely castle.

"Who lives there?" he asked.

"A beautiful princess," he was told. "Are you one of her suitors? She plays a curious game of hide-and-seek with all who come, and says she will marry the first man who hides so well that she cannot find him."

The fisherman's son thought he would try, so boldly he went to the castle and asked to see the princess. She was indeed very beautiful, and he thought what a fine thing it would be if he could marry her.

"Princess, I will endeavour to hide where you cannot find me, but will you give me four chances?"

The princess was intrigued by this shabby boy, and agreed, thinking she would at least have some fun looking for him.

The fisherman's son went straightaway to the place where he had last seen the fish and, taking the fishbone from his pocket, he called its name.

"I am here," said the great red fish. "What can I do for you?"

"Can you take me where the princess will never find me? If you do, I shall be able to marry her."

The red fish took the boy on its back and swam deep down into the sea to some caverns where it hid him.

Now the princess had a magic mirror which she used in her games of hide-and-seek. With it she could see far and wide even through houses and hillsides. She looked in her mirror, but could not find the fisherman's son. "What a wizard he must be," she said to herself, as she turned her mirror this way and that. Then she saw him sitting in a rocky cavern deep down under the sea and she laughed.

The next day when the boy came to the palace she smiled and said, "That was easy. You were deep down in a cavern under the sea. You will have to do better than that if you are going to marry me!"

"What an enchantress she must be," said the boy to himself, and he resolved to win this contest.

He went next to the forest and held out the stag's hair and called. When the stag came he told it that he wanted to hide in a place where the princess would never find him. The stag took him on its back far far away to the other side of the mountains and hid him in a little cave. The stag then stood in front of the cave so that no one could see inside.

Once more the princess took out her mirror and searched far and wide for the boy. "How clever he is," she said to herself, and then the mirror picked him out hiding in the cave.

The next day she said to the boy, "Pooh! It was easy to see you in that cave." The boy became even more determined to marry her.

Now he set out to summon the crane, who came as soon as the boy waved the feather and called its name. He asked the crane to hide him faraway somewhere.

"Come with me high up into the clouds and the sky," said the crane, and took the boy on its back. All day long they hovered in the sky, while the princess searched this way and that in her mirror.

Just as she was about to give up, she spied him above her. "He is cleverer than I thought!" she said to herself.

But the next day when the boy came to the castle, she laughed and said, "You thought I would never find you among the clouds, but I spotted you easily. You only have one more chance to outwit me!"

The boy now went to the forest and, holding up the fox's hair he called the fox. When it came he explained what he wanted. "Ask her to give you fourteen days," said the fox, "and I should be able to hide you where she cannot find you."

The princess agreed, and for fourteen days the fox tunnelled and dug beneath the princess's castle until it had made a hole large enough for the boy to hide in right under the princess's room. Down he went and lay there quietly.

The princess took out her mirror and searched. She looked to the north, to the south, to the east, to the west, she looked high and low, round and round, and at last, exasperated, she called out,

"I give up. Where are you, fisherman's son?"

"Here I am," he called, from directly underneath her, and he jumped out from the hole the fox had dug.

"You win, wizard," she said, and was happy to marry the fisherman's son.

He was more than happy to marry the beautiful princess. They had a great wedding in the castle, and the celebrations went on for many days and nights.

E FROG PRINCE

beautiful princess who had long dark hair
which shone when she smiled, which she
a very happy person. She lived in a large
she could possibly want. But her favourite
ball. She carried it everywhere, throwing
nd catching it again.

red through the palace gardens to a quiet
old well. She sat on the edge of the well,
own and laughing with pleasure to see it
nce the golden ball slipped through her
vell with a splash.

" the princess cried, and her laughter
the water was very deep and did not
r ball back.

d a croaky voice nearby. "Good. A
she thought. "It's funny that I didn't

FERRARI TESTAROSA

The princess looked around. No gardener appeared. Then she heard the voice again. "It's coming from inside the well," she decided. As she peered into the water, out jumped a frog which sat down beside her.

"If I go to the bottom of the well and fetch your golden ball, will you promise to let me eat at your table, sleep in your bed and will you kiss me, if I want you to, Princess?" asked the frog.

The princess was so upset about losing her ball that she did not think it odd that a frog was talking to her. Instead she thought, "How ridiculous! A frog could never get into the dining hall in the palace or up to my bedroom. But it might be able to rescue my golden ball for me."

So aloud she said, "Yes, Frog, I promise to do those things if you will bring my ball back to me."

The frog disappeared into the water and returned a few moments later with the golden ball in its mouth.

"Oh, thank you," said the princess. Snatching the ball, she ran quickly back to the palace for it was nearly time for dinner. She was so pleased to have the golden ball back that she forgot all about her promises to the frog.

As the princess, the king, and all the court were eating their meal, a curious noise was heard outside the dining hall. When the door was opened, the frog jumped right inside past the servants. The princess looked at it in dismay, and the king said crossly,

"Is this one of your jokes, bringing a frog into the palace?"

"No, father," she replied. "It's not a joke. This frog has come

in by itself, but I promised that it could."

"A promise made must always be kept, my daughter," said the king solemnly. "What exactly did you promise?"

"Well, that it should eat at my table," said the princess, not mentioning the other promises. So the king told one of the servants to bring up another chair to the table and place a silken cushion on it for the frog. But the frog jumped onto the princess's lap and started to eat from her plate. The princess tried very hard not to think about how cold and damp it was. But really she found it very unpleasant sharing her food with the frog.

That evening as she was getting ready for bed she found the frog in her bedroom.

"Oh, Frog," she exclaimed, "I suppose now you have come to sleep in my bed. Very well, a promise made has to be kept, my father says. You may sleep on the end of my bed."

The frog, however, jumped on to her pillow and sat there, cold and damp, waiting for the princess to get into bed. Reluctantly she edged under the covers.

"Please kiss me," then croaked the frog.

Now the princess did not want to break her word, nor did she want to kiss the frog. "If I do it quickly, that should be all right," she decided. As her lips touched the frog's smooth skin, she felt it change. Suddenly there before her was a handsome young man.

"Thank you," he cried, "thank you for releasing me from the spell a wicked witch put on me. She turned me into a frog, and told me the spell would only be broken if a princess agreed to let me eat at her table, sleep in her bed and then kiss me. I am a prince from a neighbouring country and I have waited a long, long time to find a princess who could break the spell."

"Let us go down and tell my father," said the princess.

The king was delighted when he heard the prince's story and invited him to stay for a few days. The prince had loved the princess from the moment he first saw her by the well. Before long the princess fell in love with the prince and agreed to be his bride.

They had a grand wedding and then they rode off together to their new home in the prince's country. They lived happily for many years and when the princess wished to tease her husband, she would laugh and call him her 'Frog Prince'.

WHY THE SEA IS SALT

O nce upon a time there were two brothers who lived near each other. One was rich and one was poor. One Christmas Eve the poor brother had nothing to eat in his house. There wasn't even a crust of bread and he had no money to buy any.

"My poor wife will not have a happy Christmas," he thought. "I know that my brother does not like giving things away but I'll go and ask him once more to help me."

The rich brother did not welcome him even though it was Christmas time.

"I'll give you plenty of meat if you promise to go away and never come back," he said grumpily.

"Thank you, thank you," his brother replied. "I promise I will not bother you again."

"Here is a whole side of bacon," said the rich brother. "Be off with you and mind that you go straight to the Land of Hunger."

The poor brother was very pleased and he set off with the bacon over his back. He walked all day but he didn't find the Land of Hunger. It was getting dark when he came to a village with many bright lights. "Perhaps this is what I'm looking for," he thought.

He stopped to talk to an old man with a long white beard who was gathering wood for Christmas. The old man looked up. "Good evening," he said. "You are travelling rather late on Christmas Eve, aren't you? Where are you going?"

"Well, I'm trying to find the Land of Hunger. Is this the right way?" the man carrying the bacon replied.

"Oh yes, this is the land all right," said the old man, looking at the bacon closely. "You should go over to that house. You will find that everybody will want to buy your side of bacon. We don't get much meat here. But whatever you do, don't sell it unless you can get a hand-mill in exchange. I know there is one behind the door."

"Thank you," the man replied. "But I would not know what to do with a hand-mill."

"That's easy," came the reply. "I'll teach you all about it then you will be able to grind anything you like."

The poor man was not very sure about this but he went across and knocked on the door. He went inside and as soon as the people in the room saw the bacon they wanted to buy it. Each one offered more and more money until at last the stranger held up his hand and they stopped talking at once.

"My wife and I were going to eat this bacon for our Christmas dinner. But if you want it so much I'd better let you have it. I don't want any money. Just let me have that hand-mill over there."

"We can't do that. We need it ourselves," they answered, and everybody started to argue. But in the end they wanted the bacon so much that they had to agree.

The old man was waiting outside. He kept his promise and he told the man all about the hand-mill. He showed him exactly what to do to make it grind anything he wanted.

"You have been very kind," the man thanked him. "I must hurry now as I am so late already. Goodbye and happy Christmas!"

The clock was striking midnight when he reached his door.

"Where have you been?" His wife started to scold him. "I've been so worried, with never a bite to eat. There's no wood either to light a fire to warm the house and not a scrap of food in the cupboard."

"Never mind," her husband replied. "I have had many things to do and I've been a very long way today. But here I am safe and sound, dear wife. Now watch and see what happens!" and he put the hand-mill on the table.

"Grind lights!" he ordered. At once there were candles shining everywhere. "Grind a tablecloth!" A snow-white cloth appeared. Now the husband asked the mill for meat, bread, milk and presents until the cottage was filled with good things. The mill went on grinding whatever they wanted, day or night.

"What a lovely Christmas this will be. How lucky we are!" the wife said at last. "But where did you get this wonderful mill?"

"Please don't bother me with a lot of questions," her husband

joked, "but let us enjoy our good fortune." Then he ordered the mill to grind enough food to last until Twelfth Night. "It would be very nice to have a party," he thought.

So on the third day after Christmas he asked all his relatives and neighbours to come to his house for a feast. When his rich brother arrived he was very surprised at all the changes in his brother's house. He was very angry and jealous as well.

"My brother came begging for food on Christmas Eve," he started shouting. "He had no food and no money. Now he is giving a feast like this! Does he think he is the king? Where did all these things come from, I should like to know."

"Oh, they came from here and there," the owner of the mill said. "It's just my little secret." The feasting went on all night and the older brother went on asking so many questions, that in the end the younger brother couldn't keep his secret to himself any longer.

"Here is my secret," he said proudly. "This little mill has made me a rich man." He made the mill grind a valuable present for each of his friends to show them how it worked.

Well, this made the elder brother even angrier for he hated to see anyone else getting rich. He wanted that mill very much so he begged his brother to sell it to him. In the end, he was forced to hand over a large bag of gold and in return his brother agreed to give up the mill at harvest-time. That mill worked very hard for the next few months because the younger brother filled his house with enough money and treasure to last him and his wife for many years.

At last harvest-time came and the rich brother couldn't wait to get his hands on the mill. He was in such a hurry to take it away that he didn't find out *all* about it.

The next day he and his wife got up as usual. "You go into the fields today and help to toss the hay," he said after breakfast. "I'll stay and get dinner ready if you like." He was very pleased when it was almost dinner-time so that he could try out the mill. He put it on the table in the kitchen.

"Grind herrings and broth! Grind them at once and grind them well!" He ordered. At once the mill began to grind out herrings and broth. They filled every bowl and dish in the house. Then they filled the pans and all the big tubs. When these were full, they overflowed all over the kitchen floor and the table and chairs started to float. The man grabbed the mill. He twisted it this way and that to make it stop. He banged it and he shouted at it but it went on grinding out herrings and broth. This soon flooded the kitchen and the man was almost drowning while he tugged and pulled at the kitchen door. It opened at last and he ran to the sitting-room. He thought he was safe there but soon the mill had ground enough broth and herrings to flood all the rooms downstairs. Quickly he swam to the front door and he managed to pull it open just as his breath had almost finished.

He ran across the farmyard and down the road. But the mill kept on grinding. Herrings and broth followed him over the yard in a roaring flood.

Out in the fields his wife started to feel hungry. "It must be dinner-time!" she called to the farm workers who were tossing hay with her. "I think we'll go home now. Perhaps the master hasn't been able to cook the broth! I expect he needs my help."

The men were hungry too so they all set off together. As they

were going up the hill, they heard a lot of strange noises. Then
they saw herrings and broth bubbling, splashing and spluttering
and rushing towards them. The master was racing along in front
of this thick stream. He could not stop in case he drowned. He
yelled at his wife and the workers. "We need a thousand mouths
to drink this soup. Get out of the way or you'll be drowned!"

He went on running until he reached his brother's house.

"Stop this thing from grinding," he begged. "If you don't the
whole village will be flooded by these herrings and broth. And you
can take back this horrid mill at once."

"Certainly," the other brother said calmly. "But you must
give me another bag of gold."

"Anything, I'll give you anything. Just stop this flood!" So the
younger brother now had more gold and he had the mill back
again.

He and his wife decided to build a big house near the sea. He
asked the mill to grind enough gold to cover all the outside walls.
Sailors said the glistening gold house was as good as a lighthouse
for they could see it from their ships far out on the sea.

One day, a sea-captain sailed into the harbour. He went to
see the famous house and the mill.

"Can it grind salt?" he asked.

"Salt!" said the owner. "This mill can grind anything."

"I'd like to buy your mill. What's your price?" he asked.

"I can't give it up," came the reply. "It's just like an old friend now." The captain begged him to change his mind and after some time the man agreed to sell the mill for a big bag of gold.

The sea-captain set off at once with the mill on his back and he and his sailors set sail for the open seas. The captain sailed his ship to the middle of the sea, then he carried the mill up on deck from his cabin.

"Open all the doors to the store-rooms, men!" he ordered. "Now," he said. "Grind salt! Grind at once and grind it fast!" At once the mill obeyed the order. White and glittering salt poured out. It flowed smoothly like a river into all the empty store-rooms. Then the cook came running up on deck.

"There's salt all over the galley," he wailed.

"I can't turn this wheel," called the sailor who was steering the ship. "There's salt all round it!"

The captain shouted at the mill to stop grinding. But salt kept pouring out. He pulled and tugged at it. His sailors pulled and tugged – one even gave it a kick, but no matter what they did or how hard they tried, that mill kept grinding away. The salt had now covered all the decks and the sailors could not walk properly over them.

"Lower the lifeboats!" cried the captain suddenly. "Hurry, men." He could see that there was so much salt on his ship that it was sinking! The lifeboats reached the water just in time. The sailors were safe but their ship sank in front of their eyes. They watched as the mill floated on the waves for a few minutes then it sank as well. It went to the bottom of the sea but it didn't stop grinding. It goes on day after day grinding away and that is why the sea is salt.

THE OSSOPIT TREE

One terribly hot summer in the forests of Africa there was a great shortage of anything to eat. The animals had been hunting around here, there and everywhere and had finally eaten up the very last twig and root. They were very hungry indeed.

Suddenly they came upon a wonderful-looking tree, hung with the most tempting, juicy-looking fruit. But, of course, they didn't know whether the fruit was safe to eat or not because they had no idea what its name was. And they simply had to know its name.

Luckily they did know that the tree belonged to an old lady called Jemma. So they decided to send the hare, their fastest runner, to ask her what the name of the tree was.

Off went the hare as fast as his legs could carry him and he found old Jemma in front of her hut.

"Oh, Mrs Jemma," he said. "We animals are dying of hunger. If you could only tell us the name of that wonderful tree of yours you could save us all from starving."

"Gladly I will do that," answered Jemma. "It's perfectly safe to eat the fruit. Its name is OSSOPIT."

"Oh," said the hare. "That's a very difficult name. I shall forget it by the time I get back."

"No, it's really quite easy," said Jemma. "Just think of 'opposite' and then sort of say it backwards, like this:

opposite – OSSOPIT."

"Oh, thanks very much," said the hare, and off he scampered.

As he ran he kept muttering, "Opposite, ottipis, ossipit" and he got all mixed up. So that when he got back to the other animals all he could say was:

"Well, Jemma did tell me the name but I can't remember whether it's ossipit, ottipis, or ossupit. I do know it's got something to do with 'opposite'."

"Oh dear," they all sighed. "We had better send someone with a better memory."

"I'll go," said the goat. "I never forget anything." So he headed straight for Jemma's hut, grunting and snorting all the way.

"I'm sorry to bother you again, Mrs Jemma," he panted, "but that stupid hare couldn't remember the name of the tree. Do you mind telling it me once more?"

"Gladly I will," replied the old woman. "It's OSSOPIT. Just think of 'opposite' and then sort of say it backwards:

opposite – OSSOPIT."

"Rightee-oh," said the goat, "and thank you very much, I'm sure."

And off he galloped, fast as he could, kicking up clouds of dust, and all the way he kept saying:

"Ottopis, oppossit, possitto, otto . . ." until he got back to the other animals.

"I know the name of that tree," he said. "It's oppitis, n . . . no

. . . ossipit, n . . . no . . . otup . . . oh dear . . . I just can't get it right."

"Well, who can we send this time?" they all asked. They didn't want to bother old Jemma again.

"I'm perfectly willing to have a go," piped up a young sparrow. "I'll be back in no time," and with a whisk of his tail he had flown off before anyone could stop him.

"Good morrow, gentle Jemma," he said. "Could you please tell me the name of that tree just *once* more. Hare and goat could *not* get it right."

"Right gladly I will," said old Jemma patiently. "It's osso-PIT, OSS-O-PIT. It's a wee bit difficult but just think of 'opposite' and then sort of say it backwards:

opposite – OSSOPIT."

"I'm most grateful, madam," said the sparrow and flew off twittering to himself: "Opposite, ossitup, ottupus, oissopit," until he finally got back to his famishing friends.

"Do tell us, sparrow," they all cried.

"Yes," chirped the sparrow. "It's definitely 'ossitup', n . . . no . . . oittuisip, n . . . no . . . oippisuit . . . Oh dear, I give up. So very sorry."

By now the animals were desperate. Just imagine them all sitting round the gorgeous tree and unable to pick any of its mouth-watering fruits.

Suddenly up spoke the tortoise. "I shall go," he said. "I know it will take a bit of time but I will not forget the name once I've been told. My family has the finest reputation in the world for good memories."

"No," they moaned. "You are too slow. We shall all be dead by the time you get back."

"Why not let me take tortoise on my back?" asked the zebra. "I'm hopeless at remembering things but my speed is second to none. I'll have him back here in no time at all." They all thought this was a splendid idea and so off raced the zebra with the tortoise clinging to his back.

"Good morning, Madam Jemma," said the tortoise. "I'm sorry I have no time to alight. But if we don't get the name of that tree most of us will be dead by tonight. That's why I've come on zebra's back. He's a bit faster than I am, you know."

"Yes, I rather think he is," smiled old Jemma benignly.

"Well, it's OSSOPIT. Just think of 'opposite' and then sort of say it backwards, like this: opposite – oss-o-pit."

"Just let me repeat it three times before I go," said the tortoise, "just to see if I get it right." And then he said it, very, very slowly, deliberately and loudly, and nodding his tiny head at each syllable:

"OSS-O-PIT, OSS-O-PIT, OSS-O-PIT."

"Bravo!" said Jemma, "you'll never forget it now."

And she was right.

The zebra thudded back hot foot and the tortoise was never in any doubt that he had the name right at last.

"It's OSS-O-PIT," he announced to his ravenous friends.

"Ossopit, ossopit, ossopit," they all cried. "It's an ossopit tree, and it's perfectly safe to eat." And they all helped themselves to the wonderful fruit. You just can't imagine how delicious it tasted.

And to show how grateful they were, they appointed the tortoise their Chief Adviser on Important Matters (he has C.A.I.M. after his name). And he still is Chief Adviser to this very day.

THE HALF-LIE

One day a rich merchant was walking through the market in Cairo. He saw a strong young slave for sale.

"How much do you want for this one?" he asked.

"He is very cheap," said the slave owner. "I am only asking five hundred silver coins for him. You see, there is one thing wrong with him."

"What is that? Is it very bad?" asked the merchant.

"Well," the slave owner said. "His name is Kafur and he always tells one lie a year. If you buy him, you must watch out for this."

The merchant thought he was getting a bargain, five hundred silver coins for a slave! So he bought Kafur. "One lie a year isn't much," he decided, "I tell more than that myself!"

Kafur worked very well for months. He was happy and everybody liked him.

On New Year's Day the merchant and some friends rode on their mules to a lovely garden outside the city. They took carpets to sit on and baskets of fruit and wine which Kafur helped to carry. They enjoyed themselves very much, then the merchant called Kafur to his side and told him to ride home for more fruit.

Kafur did as he was ordered. But when he got to the city he started to wail and shout. He tore his long robe for that is what people did at that time to show they were unhappy.

"Oh my poor master," Kafur shouted. "Oh dear, what will happen to his family now?" He went on shouting and crying until many people came out of their houses to listen. They followed Kafur to his master's house.

"Whatever is the matter?" called the merchant's wife, as she ran to the door.

"Oh, my poor mistress," Kafur answered. "The master is dead. He was sitting with his friends in the garden. Suddenly a big wall fell down on top of them. They were all killed."

He started to cry, so did the merchant's wife. So did her children and the other servants in the house. The wife tore her dress. Then she ran round the house and she started to break the windows. People did this as well in those days, to show how upset they were.

"Come along, Kafur," the poor wife said. "Help me to be sad." They pulled down the curtains and rubbed dust on the walls. They kicked open the cupboards and broke all the cups and saucers. Crash. That was a lovely blue vase broken into pieces. Bang! And Kafur threw a large pile of plates through the window. He hurled a pretty little table after the plates and it crashed into the garden below.

"Oh, my poor master. My dear good master," he cried and at each shout, he broke something else. The merchant's wife ripped

open the silk cushions. She tore the sofas and chairs. She and Kafur moved into the kitchen and soon every single green, pink and blue bowl was smashed. Not a single piece of china was left, so they tossed valuable gold and silver goblets against the windows which broke into a thousand pieces. The noise was tremendous and all the time Kafur kept calling out, "My poor master! Oh mistress, what will happen to us now?"

Before long the lovely house was wrecked. There was soot from the fireplace on the walls: broken china and glass over the floors and not a single chair fit to sit on.

"We must go and fetch my poor dear husband's body now," the wife said. She burst into tears. So did her children and the servants. Women followed to help her then more and more neighbours joined them so there was a long procession. One of the neighbours ran to tell the sad news to the governor of the city. He sent workmen with shovels so that they could help to dig out the bodies of the merchant and his friends. There was a huge crowd now which could only move slowly along. Kafur was at the front still wailing and weeping: "Oh my poor master!"

He walked quickly ahead and then he started to run so that he got to the garden first. He still cried but now he was shouting: "Oh my poor mistress! My dear sweet mistress! What will become of us now?"

The merchant looked up. "What's this? What are you saying?"

"Oh master, you must be brave," Kafur said. "When I got to your house it had completely fallen down. All the people inside were killed."

"What about my wife?" asked the merchant.

"Dead," wailed Kafur.

"My lovely children?"

"Dead," wailed Kafur.

"And my favourite mule, the one I always ride?"

"Completely crushed," wailed Kafur. "All the animals were crushed. Not a hen or a sheep or a goat was left alive."

It was the merchant's turn to weep and to tear his long silken robe. His friends heard Kafur's story and they started to weep and to tear their clothes as well. Then they packed up sadly and started to walk back to the city.

Of course, about halfway along the road they met the merchant's wife and family, her servants, her kind neighbours and the workmen with their shovels, all ready to dig out some bodies.

"Oh my dear husband, how did you escape?" cried the merchant's wife.

"My sweet wife, are you quite safe?" cried the merchant.

"Of course we are," said his wife. "Kafur came to the house crying and shouting. He told us that the garden wall had fallen down and you and your friends had been killed."

"Oh no!" said the merchant. "Kafur came to me. He said our house had crashed down and that all of you were dead!"

Everybody turned their eyes on Kafur. He stood there still tearing his robe and making a lot of crying noises. "What is all this, you miserable slave?" demanded the merchant. You must indeed be wicked for you have caused much sadness. Wait until I get you home. You'll get a beating that you will never forget, I promise you."

Kafur started to laugh. "Oh master, that's not fair," he said. "You only paid five hundred silver coins for me though I'm worth much more. I'm a good servant even if I have one big fault. You said that you didn't mind if I told one lie a year and so far I've only told half a lie. I'll tell the other half-lie before the New Year comes."

The merchant was very angry at these words. But the crowds agreed with Kafur. It would not be fair for him to be punished.

They went on to the house, and when the merchant saw his broken treasures he said to Kafur:

"Did you say this happened because of a *half*-lie?"

"Yes, my master."

"Well, one half-lie ruined my house, so a whole lie might wreck a city! You're not going to tell the other half here, my boy. I give you your freedom here and now. Leave my house at once."

This meant that Kafur was not a slave any more. He could work anywhere. Alas, people remembered the trouble he had caused with a half-lie and in the end nobody would give him a job. He ended his days as a beggar in the streets.

TALES OF BRER RABBIT

U ncle Remus was an old man who loved to tell stories about animals. Mostly he spun yarns about Brer Rabbit and Brer Fox and how more often than not Brer Rabbit got the better of Brer Fox.

One evening when the lady, whom Uncle Remus called Miss Sally, was looking for her little boy, she heard the sound of voices in the old man's cabin, and she saw the boy sitting by Uncle Remus. He was telling a story and this is how it began:

One hot summer day Brer Rabbit, Brer Fox, Brer Coon, Brer Bear and the other animals were clearing some ground so that it could be planted for the next year. The sun got hot and Brer Rabbit got tired. But he kept on working because he feared the others would call him lazy. Suddenly he hollered out that he had a thorn in his hand and he slipped off to find a cool place to rest. After a while he came across a well with two buckets hanging over it.

"That looks cool," says Brer Rabbit to himself, "I'll just get in there and take a nap," and with that, in he jumped. He was no sooner in one bucket than it began to drop down the well.

There has never been a more scared creature than Brer Rabbit at this moment. Almost straightaway he felt the bucket hit the water and there it sat. And Brer Rabbit, he kept as still as he could and just lay there and shook and shivered.

Now Brer Fox always had one eye on Brer Rabbit, and when he slipped off, Brer Fox sneaked after him and watched. He knew Brer Rabbit was up to something. Brer Fox saw Brer Rabbit come to the well, and he saw him jump in the bucket and then, lo and behold, he saw the bucket go down the well, out of sight.

Brer Fox was the most astonished fox that you ever laid eyes on. He sat there in the bushes and thought and thought but could not make head nor tail of what was going on.

Then he said to himself, "Right down in that well is where

Brer Rabbit keeps his money hidden. If that's not it, then he's discovered a gold mine. I'm going to see what's in there."

Brer Fox crept a little nearer, but he heard nothing. So he crept nearer again and still heard nothing. Then he got right up close and peered down into the well, but he could see nothing.

All this time Brer Rabbit was lying in the bucket scared out of his skin. If he moved the bucket might tip over and spill him out into the water. As he was saying his prayers, old Brer Fox hollered out, "Heyo, Brer Rabbit, who are you visiting down there?"

"Who? Me? Oh, I'm just fishing, Brer Fox," says Brer Rabbit. "I just said to myself I'd sort of surprise you with a lot of fishes for dinner, so here I am, and here are all the fishes. I'm fishing for suckers, Brer Fox," says Brer Rabbit.

"Are there many down there, Brer Rabbit?" says Brer Fox.

"Lots of them, Brer Fox. Scores and scores of them. The water is alive with them. Come down and help me haul them in, Brer Fox," says Brer Rabbit.

"How am I going to get down, Brer Rabbit?"

"Jump into the bucket, Brer Fox. It will bring you down safe and sound."

Brer Rabbit sounded so happy that Brer Fox jumped into the other bucket and it began to fall. As he went down into the well, his weight pulled Brer Rabbit's bucket up. When they passed one another, half way up and half way down, Brer Rabbit called out,

> *"Goodbye Brer Fox, take care of your clothes,*
> *For this is the way the world goes,*
> *Some goes up and some goes down,*
> *You'll get to the bottom all safe and sound."*

Brer Rabbit's bucket reached the top of the well and he jumped out. He galloped off to the people who owned the well and told them that Brer Fox was down the well muddying their drinking water. Then he galloped back to the well and hollered down to Brer Fox,

> *"Here comes a man with a great big gun,*
> *When he hauls you up, you jump and run."*

"What then, Uncle Remus?" asked the little boy quickly, as the old man paused.

"My oh my," replied Uncle Remus, "in about half an hour both of them were back on the ground that was being cleared, working as though they'd never heard of any well, except every now and then Brer Rabbit burst out laughing. And old Brer Fox, he looked mighty sore."

The next evening the little boy had more questions,

"Didn't the Fox ever catch the Rabbit?" he asked Uncle Remus.

"He came mighty near it, honey, sure as you're born," replied Uncle Remus, "and this is how it happened."

One day Brer Fox got some tar and mixed it with some turpentine and fixed up a contraption which he called a Tar-Baby. He took this Tar-Baby and sat her in the road and then he lay in the bushes to see what was going to happen. He did not have to wait long because by and by along came Brer Rabbit all dressed up as fine as a jay-bird. Brer Rabbit pranced along *lippity-clippity, clippity-lippity* until he spied the Tar-Baby. He stopped in astonishment. The Tar-Baby just sat there and Brer Fox, he lay low.

"Morning!" says Brer Rabbit. "Nice weather this morning!" he says. But the Tar-Baby said nothing and Brer Fox, he lay low.

"Are you deaf?" says Brer Rabbit, "For if you are, I can holler louder."

The Tar-Baby stayed still and Brer Fox, he lay low.

"You're stuck up, that's what you are," shouts Brer Rabbit. "I'm going to teach you how to talk to respectable folks. If you don't take that hat off, I'll hit you."

But of course the Tar-Baby stayed still and Brer Fox, he lay low. Brer Rabbit drew back his fist and *blip*, he hit the side of the Tar-Baby's head. His fist stuck and he couldn't pull loose.

"If you don't let me loose I'll hit you again," says Brer Rabbit, and he swiped at the Tar-Baby with his other hand and that stuck too.

"Let me loose before I kick the stuffing out of you," hollers Brer Rabbit.

But the Tar-Baby said nothing. She just held on and Brer

Rabbit soon found his feet stuck in the same way. Then he butted the Tar-Baby with his head and that stuck too.

Now Brer Fox sauntered out of the bushes, looking as innocent as a mocking-bird.

"Howdy, Brer Rabbit," he says, "you look sort of stuck up this morning," and he rolled on the ground with laughter. He laughed and laughed until he could laugh no more.

"And Brer Rabbit," Uncle Remus finished with a chuckle, "he was stuck as tight as tight could be."

The very next evening the little boy asked Uncle Remus sadly whether the Fox killed and ate the Rabbit when he caught him with the Tar-Baby.

"Now now, honey," said Uncle Remus, "don't you go crying over Brer Rabbit. You wait and see how he ends up." And he went on with the story.

As Brer Rabbit struggled on the ground with the Tar-Baby, Brer Fox crowed triumphantly,

"Hah! I've got you this time and it's your own fault. No one asked you to strike up an acquaintance with the Tar-Baby. You just stuck yourself on to it, and now I'm going to make a fire and barbecue you."

Then Brer Rabbit began to talk in a very humble voice.

"I don't care," he says, "what you do with me as long as you don't throw me in that briar patch. Roast me, but don't throw me in the briar patch."

"It's so much trouble to kindle a fire, I think I'll hang you or drown you," says Brer Fox.

"Hang me as high as you please, drown me as deep as you please, Brer Fox, but don't fling me in that briar patch."

Now Brer Fox wanted to hurt Brer Rabbit as much as possible. So he picked him up by the hind legs and slung him right into the middle of the briar patch. He then waited to see what would happen next.

Suddenly he heard someone calling him. Way up the hill was Brer Rabbit sitting cross-legged on a log, combing tar out of his fur. Then Brer Fox knew he'd been tricked, and just to rub it in Brer Rabbit called out,

"Bred and born in a briar patch, Brer Fox, bred and born in a briar patch."

"With that he skipped off as lively as a cricket," said Uncle Remus, "and lived to trick Old Brer Fox another day."

JEROME, THE LION AND THE DONKEY

Jerome was a holy man who lived in a monastery many hundreds of years ago. One hot afternoon, he and some of the other monks were sitting together, when a lion appeared in the courtyard of the monastery. There was panic and confusion as several of the monks thought the lion had come to kill them, but Jerome saw that one of the lion's paws was swollen and the lion was limping.

"Calm yourselves, brothers," he said, "and bring me some clean cloths and warm water. The poor creature has come to us for help. We need not be afraid of him."

Cautiously they gathered round, and one man fetched warm water, another a clean cloth for a bandage, and another some ointment made from healing herbs. Very gently, and with great care, Jerome knelt by the lion, and first bathed and then bound up the torn foot. The lion had obviously been in great pain but he seemed much better after the treatment and lay down peacefully in the shade of the courtyard and slept.

The next day the lion was still there, and so Jerome bathed his paw again. It looked cleaner and less swollen, and the lion seemed grateful for the help he had received. So it was for several days, until the paw was completely healed.

Most of the monks had overcome their fear of having a lion in the monastery, but nonetheless they were pleased to hear he was cured, as they thought he would now go away.

But the lion did not go. He stayed and followed Jerome when he went to work in the fields, and lay down in the courtyard when Jerome was in the monastery. Several monks felt certain that a fully grown lion, no longer in pain, must be savage, and that sooner or later someone would be hurt. However, when they tried sending the lion away – even when Jerome left him in the woods himself – he always came back to the monastery.

"It's no good," said Jerome. "He has come to stay."

"It is not right that he should stay for he does no work," said one of the monks. "None of us stays here without working."

So Jerome said, "Well, let us think of some work he can do."

Then one old monk whose job it was to take the donkey to the woods every day to collect logs for the fire, said, "Let the lion go with the donkey each day. He will stop wild beasts attacking the donkey better than I can, and I will then be free to do other jobs in the monastery."

So it was agreed, and each day the lion and the donkey set out together for the woods. On the way the donkey would eat grass in the pasture while the lion guarded him. The woodmen would then fill the baskets that were strapped to the donkey's back with logs, and together they would return.

"What a useful member of the community he is," said some of the monks, while others still took care not to get too close in case the lion turned savage.

One day, as the donkey was grazing, the lion found a shady spot to lie and wait for his friend, and in the still of the hot day he dropped off to sleep. As he slept some travelling merchants with a string of camels came by, and saw the donkey grazing alone.

"Look at that," they said to each other. "A donkey is just what we want to lead our camels. No one seems to be looking after it. Let's take it quickly."

Now the merchants, although they could see no one, knew they were stealing, for the donkey had baskets on his back and obviously belonged to someone, but they reckoned they would be over the border into a different country by nightfall, and nobody would ever know where the donkey had gone. They threw the baskets behind a bush, and led him off at the head of their string of camels.

When the lion awoke and found the donkey had disappeared, he roared in misery, and returned that evening to the monastery his head hanging low with shame. The monks crowded round him, some of them saying,

"A wild beast should never be trusted. He has killed and eaten our dear donkey, even after all these months of appearing to be such a gentle animal."

Jerome said, "Do not judge him too quickly, brothers. Let us

go to the wood and see if we find something to show us what happened to the donkey."

So a group of monks set off, and when they found the donkey's baskets, they said, "Look, here is the evidence we wanted. This shows the donkey was killed by the savage lion."

But the lion still showed no sign of being fierce, so Jerome suggested to the angry monks that since the lion was obviously at fault, in that he had failed to guard the donkey, he should now do the donkey's work.

"Let him go to the woods each day with the donkey's baskets strapped to his back," he said, "and let him carry the logs we need as the little donkey used to do."

The monks agreed to Jerome's plan, and each morning after that the lion set out for the woods alone, with the donkey's baskets strapped to his back.

A whole year went by, and during this time Jerome was made the head monk in the monastery because his wisdom and his gentleness were respected by all. The lion, still Jerome's friend and companion, continued to go each day to get wood for the monastery. He did the task without complaining, almost as if he were saying, "I am sorry about the donkey," each time they strapped the baskets on him.

One day, when he was padding gently to the woods, he caught sight of his old friend the donkey. The travelling merchants were once more on their old route and the little donkey they had stolen was leading their string of camels. Without hesitating, the lion gave a great roar and bounded over to the donkey. The merchants, thinking they were being attacked by a wild and ferocious lion, fled in terror, while the donkey gave a bray of delight and trotted over to his friend the lion.

Together they set off towards the monastery, for the lion wished to show the monks that he had found the little donkey. For a whole year the camels had followed the donkey, and now they continued to do so. The merchants were all hiding and could do nothing to stop them. So the monks looked up in astonishment to see the strange procession of lion, donkey and camels coming into the courtyard.

"I see," said Jerome, "that the lion has made good his fault. He has found the donkey he so carelessly lost a year ago. We have been harsh to doubt him, and to think he might have killed the donkey."

Just then the courtyard was filled with angry merchants who had followed the camels. Now they asked to speak to the head of the monastery, and Jerome stepped forward.

90

"You have stolen our donkey, our camels and all our wares," they shouted angrily. "We demand you return them at once."

"We have stolen nothing," Jerome replied quietly. "Your camels and the goods they carry are yours to take away. The camels came here of their own accord. But the donkey is not yours to take. He was ours, and he was stolen last year. It must have been you who took him, and hid his baskets behind the bush. Now he has come back with his friend the lion to his real owners."

The merchants then changed their tone. "We found the donkey on its own one day. We are really very sorry," they told the monks. Promising they would not steal again and still eyeing the lion with fear, they went on their way, taking their camels and goods with them.

The donkey and the lion went out together each day as before, and the monks who had thought the lion a savage beast were sorry that they had misjudged him. The lion lived for many more years in the monastery, and in his old age he would sit at Jerome's feet as the holy man wrote books. The monastery was known far and wide as a place where wisdom and gentleness were always to be found.

NAIL SOUP

 One dark and stormy night, a tramp knocked on the door of a cottage and asked for shelter. An old woman answered the door and told the tramp sourly that he could come in if he wanted, but he must not expect any food for she had none in the house.

"And don't think you'll get a bed to sleep on either," she added, "as I only have one and that is where I sleep. You'll have to sleep on a chair."

The tramp was hungry, but he could see he wasn't going to get any food, so he sat by the fire and took an old nail out of his pocket and tossed it from hand to hand.

"Do you see this nail here?" he said at last. "You'd never believe it, but last night I made the finest soup I have ever eaten by cooking this nail, and what is more I still have it to make some more tonight. Would you like me to make you some nail soup?"

"Nail soup!" snorted the old woman. "I have never heard of such a thing. Don't talk nonsense." But the tramp could see she was curious.

"All I did," he told her, "was to boil it up in an old saucepan, and it was delicious."

"Well, since we have nothing else to do, and I have no food in the house, perhaps you would be good enough to show me how you do it," she said after a few minutes.

"You haven't a large pot and some water, have you?" asked the tramp.

"Why yes," said the old woman, handing a big cooking pot to the tramp and showing him where the water was. She watched as the tramp carefully filled the pot half full with water, placed it on the stove, and dropped in the nail. Then he sat down to wait.

From time to time, the old woman peeped into the pot to see how the soup was doing, and once when she lifted the lid the tramp said,

"Last night all that was needed was a little salt and pepper. I

92

don't suppose you have any in the house?"

"I might have," said the old woman ungraciously, and from a cupboard she took salt and pepper which she dropped into the water with the nail.

The next time she lifted the lid, the tramp sighed, "What a pity you haven't got half an onion for that would make the soup even better than it was last night."

"I think I might just have an onion," said the old woman, quite excited by now at the thought of the nail soup, and she went to the larder to fetch an onion. As she opened the door, the tramp caught a glimpse of shelves stacked with food, but he said nothing until the onion had been in the pot for about ten minutes.

Then, stirring the soup again, he murmured to himself, "How sad that this fine onion has no carrots and potatoes to go with it." Just as he had hoped, the old woman quickly fetched some carrots and potatoes from the larder, peeled and chopped them, and put them in the pot.

By now, the soup was beginning to smell good, and it was not long before the tramp said that on nights when he could add a little meat to his nail soup, it was fit even for kings and queens. In a flash, the old woman had fetched some meat and put it in the pot.

While the soup was bubbling, the tramp looked round at the table. "It's a funny thing," he remarked, "but my nail soup

93

always tastes better when I eat it at a table that is laid with pretty china and when there is a candle or two on the table.''

The old woman, not to be outdone, put out her best tablecloth and got the best china off the dresser. Soon the table looked ready for a feast.

"What a shame," said the tramp, "that we have no bread to eat with this nail soup, but I remember you telling me there is no food in the house.''

"I'll just look in the bread crock," said the old woman, and she pulled out a loaf that looked as though it had been baked that morning.

The soup now smelled quite delicious, and the tramp was longing to eat it, but he waited a few more minutes before saying,

"I am sorry there is no wine to drink with our nail soup, as I would have liked you to enjoy it with a glass of wine.''

"Just a minute," said the old woman, and she fetched a fine-looking bottle of wine from the back of a cupboard and put it on the table with two glasses.

"Now the soup is ready. I hope you enjoy it," said the tramp heartily, and he fished the nail out with a spoon and put it in his pocket before carrying the soup over to the table.

They both had a wonderful meal. After the soup, which the old woman agreed was the best she'd ever tasted, she found some cheese and other good things in the larder. They told each other many stories, laughed a lot and had a very pleasant evening indeed.

As the candles burnt low, the old woman told the tramp to go and sleep in her bed, saying that she would be quite comfortable in a chair by the fire, and so the tramp went to bed and slept soundly.

As he left the next morning, he thanked the old woman for her kindness, but she said,

"No, no, I must thank you for showing me how to make soup from an old nail.''

"It's what you add that makes the difference!" said the tramp, smiling as he walked away down the road, and he patted the nail in his pocket to make sure it was there for the next evening.

MRS SIMKIN'S BATHTUB

"Are you aware," said Mr Simkin to Mrs Simkin one morning, "that the bathtub's halfway down the stairs?"

"How very inconvenient," said Mrs Simkin, going to have a look. "How long has it been there?"

"I have no idea," said Mr Simkin. "It was in the bathroom when I went to bed last night, and now it's here, so it must have moved when we were asleep."

"Well, we shall just have to make the best of it," said Mrs Simkin. "Will you bathe first, or shall I?"

"I will," said Mr Simkin bravely.

He stepped into the bathtub. It wobbled a bit at first, but it soon settled down. Mrs Simkin fetched soap and towels, shampoo and bath salts, and arranged them nicely on the stairs. "There," she said, "it doesn't look too bad now, and if I polish the taps and scrub the feet, it should look quite smart. I'm sure none of the neighbours has a bathtub on the stairs."

Mr Simkin said she was probably right.

After a day or two they hardly noticed that the bathtub was there at all. It didn't really inconvenience them to squeeze past it when they went upstairs, and the landing smelled so pleasantly of bath salts that Mrs Simkin began to feel quite happy about it.

She invited the lady next door to have a look, but the lady next door said that she didn't approve of these modern ideas.

One morning Mr Simkin went to have his bath. "My dear!" he cried. "Come and see! The bathtub's gone!"

"Gone!" cried Mrs Simkin, leaping out of bed. "Gone where?"

"I don't know," said Mr Simkin, "but it isn't on the stairs."

"Perhaps it's back in the bathroom," said Mrs Simkin.

They went to look, but it wasn't there.

"We shall have to buy another one," said Mr Simkin as they went down to breakfast.

The bathtub was in the kitchen.

"You know, my dear," said Mr Simkin a few minutes later, "this is a much better place for a bathtub than halfway down the stairs. I quite like having breakfast in the bath."

"Yes," agreed Mrs Simkin, "I quite like it here, too. The bath towels match the saucepans."

"That's a very good point," said Mr Simkin.

One day Mr and Mrs Simkin went downstairs to find that the bathtub had moved again. It was in the living room, sitting smugly before the fire.

"Oh, I don't think I like it there," said Mrs Simkin, "but I don't suppose it will stay there very long. Once a bathtub has started to roam, it never knows when to stop."

She was quite right. The next day they found it in the cellar, with spiders in it.

One day they couldn't find the bathtub anywhere.

"What shall we do?" cried Mrs Simkin. "It's my birthday, and I did so want to use that lovely bubble bath you gave me."

"So did I," said Mr Simkin.

The lady next door came round. "Happy birthday," she said. "Did you know that your bathtub was on the front lawn?"

They all went to have a look.

There was a horse drinking out of it.

"Go away," said Mrs Simkin. "How dare you drink my bath water, you greedy creature?"

She stepped into the bathtub. The lady next door said she didn't know what the world was coming to, and she went home and locked herself indoors.

As the bubbles floated down the street, lots of people came to see what was going on. They were very interested.

They leant on the fence and watched.

They asked if they could come again.

One day when there was rather a chilly wind about, they found the bathtub in the greenhouse. Everyone was very disappointed.

"My dear," said Mr Simkin a few days later, "do you happen to know where the bathtub is today?"

"No," said Mrs Simkin, "but today's Tuesday. It's quite

often in the garage on Tuesdays."

"It isn't there today," said Mr Simkin. "I've looked everywhere."

"I do hope it hasn't gone next door," sighed Mrs Simkin. "The lady next door has no sympathy at all."

Mr Simkin went round to inquire.

The lady next door said she was of the opinion that people ought to be able to control their bathtubs.

Mr Simkin went home.

Mr Robinson from across the street rang up. "I know it's none of my business," he said, "but I thought you'd like to know that your bathtub is on the roof of your house."

Mr Simkin went up to take his bath. All the people cheered.

The bathtub seemed to like being up there, because that's where it stayed.

The people in the street had a meeting in Mr Simkin's greenhouse. They decided to have their bathtubs on the roofs of their houses, too.

All except the lady next door.

She preferred to take a shower.

HANSEL AND GRETEL

There was once a woodcutter who lived with his children at the edge of the forest. He had a son called Hansel and a daughter called Gretel. The children's mother had died when they were small, and as their father had married again they had a stepmother. The family was very, very poor indeed. Although the woodcutter worked as hard as he could, he did not earn much money and the whole family often went to bed hungry.

The children's stepmother was not at all fond of Hansel and Gretel. She hated having to make what little food there was go round four people. Often she used to suggest sending the children away, but as their father loved them he always refused.

However, one winter when the family had even less food than usual, the stepmother persuaded her husband to take the children with them deep into the forest. She planned that once they were there she and their father would pretend to go and look for firewood. But in fact they would go home, leaving the children in the forest. Reluctantly the children's father agreed.

The children upstairs in bed had not been able to go to sleep because they were still so hungry. They overheard their father and stepmother talking and Gretel began to cry.

"Don't worry, little sister," said Hansel, "I will look after you." When his father and stepmother had gone to bed he slipped outside and saw some pebbles shining white in the moonlight. Quickly he filled his pockets with these and crept back to bed.

The next morning their father told Hansel and Gretel that they were all going to the forest to collect firewood, and perhaps find some nuts for their supper. They set off together into the forest. As his father led them down first one path and then another, Hansel lagged behind and dropped pebbles from his pocket to mark the paths they walked along. When they reached a part of the forest so far from home that neither Hansel nor Gretel had been there before, the stepmother suggested the children should wait by a tree while she and their father went a little further. Hansel and Gretel were exhausted by the long walk, and sat down thankfully. In no time at all they were fast asleep.

When they awoke, they found the grown-ups had not returned. Gretel cried because she was frightened but Hansel told her how he had dropped pebbles on the paths they had come down, and how when the moon rose his pebbles would gleam in the moonlight and show them the way home. It was just as he said. As the moon shone through the trees, Hansel and Gretel were able to retrace their steps through the forest.

It was nearly dawn when they reached their home. Their father was delighted to see his children again and gave them both a big hug. The stepmother pretended to be cross with them for getting lost. But secretly she was furious that her plan to get rid of the children had failed.

As the days went by there was even less food to eat. Once more the stepmother persuaded her husband to take the children into the forest and leave them there.

"Perhaps they'll die," she said "but at least we won't have to worry about food for them."

Hansel again overheard this plan. This time he was unable to get out and pick up pebbles as the door was locked and barred.

Instead, at breakfast the next morning, he hid his crust of bread in his pocket.

As the woodcutter and his family set off into the forest, Hansel lingered behind as before and dropped crumbs where the paths divided. He planned to use them just like the pebbles to find the way home. Later the children were left to wait by a tree but their father and stepmother never returned for them. Hansel again comforted Gretel.

"We'll find our way by following the breadcrumbs I've dropped," he told her.

Once more they set out hand in hand, sure that they would be home before morning. But this time they could not find any of Hansel's markers. It was a cold winter. The birds were hungry too, and they had flown down to eat the crumbs that Hansel had dropped. Soon the children realized they were hopelessly lost in the depths of the forest and they both felt very unhappy.

They wandered for two days, hungry and frightened. Then they came suddenly to a clearing and there before them stood a pretty little house. They went closer and saw the walls were made of gingerbread, the roof of fruitcake, and the shining windows of barley sugar. Quickly the children broke bits off the house and pushed the food into their mouths. They noticed that the whole cottage was made of delicious things to eat.

"Hallo, my pretty children," said a voice behind them. "I see I have visitors. Won't you come in and join me for supper?"

The children did not know that a witch was speaking to them as they had come under her spell when they started to eat the little house. She took them indoors and gave them a wonderful meal. Then she showed them to some little white beds and soon Hansel and Gretel were fast asleep.

During the night the wicked witch took Hansel while he was asleep and locked him in a cage. In the morning Gretel found a hard crust waiting for her for breakfast and much heavy work to be done. The witch planned to fatten up Hansel, then eat him. Poor Gretel had to work harder and harder with very little to eat.

Each day the witch would pinch Hansel to see if he was plump enough to make a good meal. She was very shortsighted though, so when Hansel pushed a chicken bone without any meat on it

100

towards her instead of his finger, the witch did not notice. Hansel grew fatter and fatter but he managed to pass some food to Gretel who was treated very cruelly by the witch. Both children longed to escape, but Gretel promised never to run away without her brother.

One day the witch grew impatient. She decided she could wait no longer. She would kill Hansel that very day, and cook him in her big oven.

"Light the fire under the oven, girl!" she ordered. "Heap up the wood and make the oven really hot."

The witch rubbed her hands together. "Test the heat now," she cackled, meaning to roast Gretel first.

But the little girl was clever. "Please show me what to do. Does my head go first?"

"Stupid!" said the witch. "You put your head inside like this."

At once Gretel gave her a big push. The witch went into the oven. Gretel slammed the oven door shut and that was the end of the witch.

Quickly Gretel found the witch's keys and unlocked the cage to let Hansel out. Then they filled their pockets with gold and silver and precious stones. Taking some food as well for the journey, they set off to find their way home.

After wandering for some time they found themselves on a path they knew. Following this they soon found they were near their own home. They ran to the house and burst through the door. There they found their father sitting sadly all alone. He jumped up in astonishment. "My dear children," he said, "I thought I'd never see you again." He told them gently that their stepmother had died. He was so pleased to see his children again that they danced around with joy.

"I'll never be so unkind again," he said. "We'll share everything, even a crust."

Then the children emptied their pockets. Their father stared in amazement at all the precious jewels they had returned with. Now they had plenty of money and they would never be hungry again.

On a winter's evening the woodcutter loved to sit by the fire and listen to Hansel and Gretel as they told him the story of how they outwitted the wicked witch. They wanted for nothing now. And so the three of them lived happily together in the forest for many years.

THE TWELVE MONTHS

In a faraway land there lived a mother with her daughter Holena and her stepdaughter Marushka. Holena and her mother disliked Marushka and the two of them made her do all the work in the cottage. Week by week Marushka grew prettier. Holena was jealous of her beauty and so Holena and her mother planned to get rid of her for ever.

One wintry day when snow was lying in deep piles round the cottage, Holena called out:

"Marushka, I want some violets. They grow high up on the mountainside. They must smell sweetly and they must be freshly picked."

"Violets don't bloom in the snow. How can I find any for you?" Marushka cried.

"Don't argue with me, miserable girl. Off you go and don't come back until you've picked a big bunch of violets for me."

Her stepmother shouted at the poor girl as well as Holena, then they pushed her outside into the snow and locked the door while they laughed unkindly.

It was hard work getting to the mountain. The snow was very deep and Marushka could not see the proper path. She wandered along and soon she was lost. She was shivering and very hungry.

"I'll have to go back," she thought, "even though they'll be so angry with me."

At that moment she saw a light flickering very faintly in front of her. She kept her eyes fixed on it and climbed and climbed until she reached the top of the mountain. To her surprise she found a big bonfire blazing there. Twelve men all dressed in long white robes were sitting around it on large blocks of stone. Three were very old, three not so old, three were young and three were very young.

Marushka was frightened but as the men looked kind she went closer to the fire.

"I have lost my way and I'm so cold," she said. "May I warm myself at your cheerful fire, please?"

One man with white hair and a long beard looked up. He was the oldest man Marushka had ever seen. He carried a long white stick, and sat in the highest place.

"What are you doing climbing the mountain in the middle of winter?" he asked.

"I'm searching for violets," replied Marushka.

"Can't you see the ground is covered with snow?"

"I know," the girl said. "My stepmother and Holena ordered me to pick some on the mountain. They will be very angry if I go back without them. Please can you help me to find some?"

The old man whose name was January went across to one of the youngest men. He handed him the long wand and said, "Brother March, please take my place."

March stood up immediately. As he walked across, he waved the wand over the bonfire. Many huge flames shot up into the sky. At once the snow melted, trees were covered with leaves and there, hiding beneath the green grass, were daffodils, primroses and lovely blue violets.

"Gather them quickly," said March.

Marushka was astonished. She picked a big bunch and thanked the Months of the Year for their help. Then she rushed happily down the mountainside.

Holena and her mother were surprised to see so many beautiful flowers. Their perfume filled the whole cottage but neither said a single word of thanks.

"Where did you find them?" demanded Holena very unpleasantly.

"On the mountain top," replied Marushka truthfully.

The next day Holena called out to Marushka again.

"I have a fancy for some strawberries. Run along to the mountain and fetch me some. They must be sweet and juicy though."

"Strawberries don't grow in the snow," said the poor step-sister.

"Do as you are told, girl. Don't dare to return without a basket filled with ripe strawberries."

Then Holena, with the help of her mother, pushed Marushka out of the cottage. They locked the door in her face and laughed cruelly. Poor Marushka pushed her way through the snow to the mountain top once more. She found the blazing fire again and she

saw that the twelve Months were still sitting on their blocks of stone.

"I'm so cold, good Months," she called. "May I warm myself for a short time?"

January was the first to look up.

"What are you doing here again? What are you looking for?"

"I must find some strawberries," the girl replied.

"Strawberries in winter!" the old man exclaimed. "How foolish." Everybody smiled at this silly idea.

"I know that but Holena and her mother have ordered me to gather some. They'll be so angry if I don't find any. Please will you help me, good Months?"

January went across to a young and handsome man. He handed him his wand and said, "Brother June, please take my place."

June moved across. He waved the wand over the fire just as March had done. At once flames shot up high into the sky and the snow all around melted. She could see leaves on the trees, flowers in the fields and she heard the birds singing sweetly. In a sheltered spot ripe red strawberries were growing.

"Gather them quickly," said the Month of June.

The girl filled her basket. She remembered to thank the Months then she ran quickly back to the house.

Holena and her mother were surprised to see Marushka. They felt sure she would get lost in the deep snow, and never return. Then they saw the big red strawberries.

"Where did you get these from?" Holena demanded. "Did you buy them from somebody?" She knew that her stepsister had no money, and her face grew uglier.

"No, I found them on the mountain," the other girl replied quietly, then she went back to her work in the house.

Holena was so greedy that she gave a few strawberries to her mother then she ate the whole basketful herself! Of course she did not give a single one to Marushka.

After a few days, Holena thought of something else she wanted. She called to her stepsister again.

"I think I'd like some nice juicy red apples," she said. "Rush and fetch me some from the mountain."

"Apples! They are picked in the autumn," Marushka exclaimed. "Can't you see, Holena, that there are not even leaves on the trees outside!"

"You are so lazy!" Holena screamed. "You have nothing to do all day so get along with you. Don't bother to come back without the apples. And you'd better make sure they are red ones too."

The stepmother started shouting as well. The two of them grabbed Marushka by the arms and pushed her outside. They threw her thin cloak after her where it landed on the snow. Then they bolted the door. This time they were sure that the girl would never come back. They rubbed their hands in glee.

In the meantime Marushka struggled through the snow to the mountain top. She found the bonfire still blazing away and the twelve Months still sitting quietly on their blocks of stone wearing their long white robes.

"My cloak is full of holes and the wind is cold," Marushka said. "May I warm myself at your lovely fire?"

January lifted his head. He looked at her and said: "Why have you come up here again? What are you looking for?"

"I'm looking for apples, kind sir."

"Apples do not grow in this weather. They come after the leaves and the flowers."

"That is true, I know. But both my stepmother and her daughter told me to find a basket of apples in the mountains for them. They'll be so very angry if I don't find them. And they must be red apples too. Please can you help me once more?"

January got up and this time he went over to one of the older Months. He gave him the long wand and said almost the same words as before, "Brother September, please take my place."

As September moved round to the highest place, he waved the wand over the fire. The flames leapt to the sky once more and the snow melted. The trees were covered with leaves but they were red and gold, and squirrels hunted for nuts. Marushka saw an apple tree and she shook its branches gently. Down fell one rosy apple after another! "Thank you, dear Months," Marushka said as she

gathered them up. Then she went happily down the mountain.

Back at the cottage Holena and her mother seized the fine juicy apples. "Why didn't you pick a lot more?" they demanded. Poor Marushka! Nothing seemed to please them.

Holena and her mother decided to gather more rosy apples for themselves so they set off up the mountain and at the top they found the Twelve Months sitting on their stone seats round a blazing bonfire. Holena was cold so she pushed boldly forward and warmed her hands at the fire.

"Why have you come here?" January asked.

"That is none of your business, old man," she answered.

"We won't tell you anything," the mother added.

These rude replies made January angry. He waved his wand furiously over his head. At once the winds howled and clouds covered the sky. The twelve Months vanished. Holena and her mother were all alone in a dreadful storm. Snow fell in big flakes and covered the paths. The two of them lost their way and were never seen again!

And so Marushka was left on her own in the cottage, but she was happy and contented for nobody scolded her ever again.

ECHO AND NARCISSUS

In a sunny part of Greece there once lived a lovely young nymph called Echo. She was so fond of her own voice that she never stopped talking. One day she was out for a walk when she met Juno, the beautiful goddess of marriage.

As usual, Echo gossiped about this and that. At last Juno held up her hand.

"Your chattering has tired me out," she said. "You will not make friends or find a husband if you talk all the time."

"Who cares!" Echo interrupted. "Other people are not half as interesting as I am. And my voice is much nicer too!"

Juno was annoyed by this rude reply.

"As a punishment for your rudeness, you will lose your voice which you are so proud of," she cried. "You will never speak your own words again. From today you will repeat the last word that other people say. Go at once to the hills. Hide yourself and do not dare to show yourself unless someone calls to you."

Echo felt frightened as she ran away. She tried to speak but her voice had gone completely. Sadly she wandered off to the hills where she lived all alone.

One day a young man called Narcissus came walking nearby. He was tall and handsome and his fair skin had not been burnt by the hot sun. His black hair fell in little curls over his forehead while his eyes sparkled and shone with happiness. Echo was hiding behind a tree as Juno had commanded but she peeped out and saw him. At once she loved him and she longed for him to notice her so that he might fall in love with her.

The young man went further up the mountain and Echo followed him. He thought he heard a little noice so he stopped. He looked all around but he could not see anyone. On he climbed then he stopped. He had heard the noise again and this time he was sure that someone was following him.

"Who is there?" he said.

"There," answered Echo, repeating the last word.

"Who are you?" he cried for he could see no one.

"You," answered Echo.

"Do not jeer at me," Narcissus cried angrily.

"Me," answered poor Echo.

"Show yourself to me here," ordered Narcissus.

"Here," answered Echo and she walked towards him.

She was beautiful but Narcissus was too angry to look closely at her. When she held out her arms in a friendly, loving way he pushed her roughly away.

"What are you doing?" he said in a temper. "Why are you pretending to love me? You have been making fun of me and I expect your friends are hiding in the trees laughing at me. Go away, I tell you. Go away!" He pushed her to one side.

"Away," murmured Echo as she hid among the trees. Her heart was broken.

"If only he had been kind to me," she thought. "One day he will fall in love with someone who will not love him. Then he will know the pain of a broken heart."

Narcissus went further up the mountain and as it was a warm day he felt thirsty. He spied a pool of clear sparkling water between some rocks.

"How fortunate!" he said and he lay down to collect water in his hands to drink. As he did this, he saw a beautiful face in the water. He fell in love at first sight with himself!

"Beautiful nymph," he whispered, "will you not come out of your pool and dance with me?"

The lips of the lovely face in the water moved each time his lips moved but he could not hear any words. He stretched out his arms to touch the face but his fingers made little waves and ripples as soon as they touched the water. At once the face vanished. He quickly lifted out his fingers and he waited until the water was smooth once more. Then he knelt down to take another look. The face had come back! He smiled and he was overjoyed when the face smiled back at him.

"Please come out of the pool," he begged. He saw the lips moving again but he could not hear a sound. He begged again and again but no one stepped out of the water.

Echo had followed Narcissus up the mountain path. She heard him talking near the water but she could not see anyone there. She peeped over his shoulder and she knew at once that Narcissus was looking at his own face. She could not believe that he had fallen in love with himself! She longed to tell him what had happened but it was impossible. Her voice had gone.

Narcissus would not leave the pool. He kept putting out his arms and he begged the nymph to leap out and join him. He lay there all day and all night for he could see his reflection in the pale moonlight. He did not eat and he could not drink for he knew that the face vanished if he touched the water. He cried bitterly but his tears made the water ripple. He looked unhappy; the face looked unhappy. He became ill and the face in the water looked ill too. Echo watched sadly but there was nothing she could do.

Then one sunny morning Narcissus died. The gods and fairies were sorry for him and they changed him into a sweet-smelling spring flower which loves to grow by pools and rivers.

Poor Echo had truly loved Narcissus and she went wandering off to the hills. She pined away until there was nothing left, except a voice. You can hear her near lakes and mountain tops. She will repeat your last word if you call out but you will never ever see the lovely Echo.

ELEPHANT AND RABBIT

Elephant and Rabbit were good friends. One day they were hungry so they went to a farmer and asked him if they could work in his fields in return for some food.

"Of course," said the farmer, "but you must promise to work hard."

"Oh yes," said Rabbit eagerly. Elephant just made a grunting sound.

The farmer saw they were really hungry so he showed them what he wanted done in his fields and then he put some beans on to cook so they would be ready to eat when the work was finished. Rabbit worked hard, while Elephant did very little. He said he was too hot or that his foot was sore, and by the time Rabbit had finished his share of the work, Elephant had barely started.

"Oh dear!" thought Rabbit, "I must help Elephant or we will never get that food."

So Rabbit started on Elephant's share of the work, and still Elephant did very little. At last the work was finished.

"Now we can eat," said Rabbit, and he went over to where the beans were bubbling and boiling in the pot.

"Wait a minute," said Elephant. "I am so dirty from all that work, I must go down to the river and wash before we eat."

Now you may not know it, but elephants in those days could take off their skins. They had sixteen buttons down the front, and when these were undone an elephant could step out of its skin.

The elephant in this story went down to the river, and undid the sixteen buttons down his front, pop, pop, pop. He stepped out of his skin, folded it up and hid it under a bush. Then he rushed towards Rabbit making a tremendous roaring noise as he went. Rabbit, as you can imagine, was scared out of his wits. He ran away as fast as he could, and hid.

Elephant quickly gobbled up all the beans that were bubbling and boiling in the pot. Then he went back to the river bank to pick up his skin. He stepped back into it, did up the sixteen buttons, and sauntered back to where the beanpot was now lying empty. There was Rabbit, waiting for him.

"Now," said Elephant, "at last we can eat."

"Oh dear no," said Rabbit in tears. "While you were down by the river washing, a great monster came roaring up. I was so scared I ran away and while I was gone the monster ate up all the beans. I am afraid we shall go to bed hungry tonight." Rabbit was so flustered that he did not notice that Elephant was not particularly hungry.

The next day much the same thing happened. Rabbit worked hard all day while Elephant made one excuse after another for doing very little. In the evening Elephant once more went down to the river to wash before they ate the beans the farmer had cooked for them.

Pop, pop, pop, Elephant undid his sixteen buttons, stepped out of his skin, and rushed up again, frightening Rabbit out of his wits for the second time.

He gobbled down the beans and, when he returned in his skin, he pretended to be very cross that the monster had eaten their food again.

Rabbit, meanwhile, had begun to wonder what an elephant would look like without his skin. He knew an elephant had sixteen buttons down the front that could be undone and began to think that an elephant without its skin might look rather like the monster who had frightened him when Elephant had been down by the river. So that night before going to sleep Rabbit made a bow and arrow and hid them in the bushes.

All the next day Rabbit worked hard in the farmer's fields while Elephant made excuses. He said the stony ground hurt his feet, the flies were troubling him and the sun was too hot. These and many other things prevented him from working all day. By evening Rabbit was really hungry, and determined to eat those bubbling boiling beans himself. This time, when Elephant said he must go down to the river to wash before their meal, Rabbit took up his bow and arrow.

Pop, pop, pop, Elephant undid his buttons, stepped out of his skin and rushed into the clearing where Rabbit was waiting. *Ping!* An arrow flew from Rabbit's bow, and struck Elephant on the shoulder. If he had been wearing his skin he would hardly have noticed, but without his skin, it really hurt!

"Ow! Ow! Ow!" shrieked Elephant, forgetting he was a monster, but he got no sympathy from Rabbit.

"Go back and get your skin, you wicked elephant," said Rabbit, "and stop making such a fuss. The arrow did not hurt that much."

When Elephant came back in his skin he found Rabbit had eaten all those bubbling boiling beans. It was his turn now to go to bed hungry and the next day Rabbit made a new arrangement with the farmer. Elephant had to look for food elsewhere and, as far as I know, he never took off his skin again.

Next time you see an elephant look carefully and you will see his skin is all loose and full of folds and creases, and looks as though it could be taken off. But over the years the sixteen buttons and buttonholes must have disappeared for, however hard you look, I don't think you will ever see them.

The Twelve Dancing Princesses

Long ago there was a king who had twelve daughters. They slept in twelve beds in a long row in the one room. Every night, when they went to bed the king shut their bedroom door. He locked it himself and every morning he would unlock it. But he always found that their slippers were worn right through and full of holes. It looked as if his twelve daughters had danced in their slippers all night instead of sleeping soundly in their beds.

They would not say a word to their father about their shoes and nobody could find out where they had been. At last the king sent this message to every part of his kingdom:

"If anyone can discover where the princesses dance in the night, that man may choose any princess for his wife. He will also be the next king, whether he be a prince or a peasant." But the message also said, anyone who did not discover the girls' secret after trying for three days and three nights, would be put to death.

The first to try was a king's son. He was taken to a small room next to the one with the twelve beds, and the princesses were locked in their room as usual. He sat in a chair to keep watch but, alas, he soon fell asleep. When he awoke next day he found twelve pairs of slippers worn into holes. The princesses must have been out dancing again! The same thing happened on the second and third nights and the king ordered his head to be cut off.

Princes, nobles, beggars came to try their luck, but they all lost their heads!

One day a poor soldier came wandering through this king's country. He came to a wood where he met an old woman.

"Who are you and where are you going?" she asked.

"I'm an old soldier and I'm off to seek my fortune," he said cheerfully. "I have heard a story about twelve princesses who dance all night. Is it true that the one who finds out where they dance will win a wife and the kingdom later on?"

The woman nodded. "It's true right enough. And I can give

you some advice: first of all, you must not drink a drop of the wine that one of the princesses will bring you in the evening. When she thinks you have finished it she will leave you and you must pretend to fall asleep.''

"It is very kind of you to tell me this. Thank you very much."

The old woman then pulled out a little cloak and handed it to him. "You will become invisible the moment you wear this cloak. You will be able to follow the princesses wherever they go."

"Where is that?" he asked.

"You must find that out yourself!" With these words she vanished.

And so the soldier set off towards the palace where the king greeted him kindly. When evening came he was taken to the room next to the one where the princesses slept. He was settling himself comfortably to keep watch when the eldest princess came in. She carried a cup of wine and she chatted about many different things. The soldier took the cup and thanked her but while she chatted, he managed to pour the wine away secretly. He did not

touch or spill a single drop. He yawned and lay back in the beautiful bed then after a little while he started to snore. He snored very loudly indeed just as if he were fast asleep.

The princesses had been pretending to go to sleep as well but as soon as they heard the soldier's loud snores they laughed merrily and then jumped out of bed and started to open cupboards and boxes. They took out their fine clothes and with much chattering and rushing about, they dressed in front of a huge looking-glass. They put on their new dancing shoes which the king had to buy for them every single day and they practised little dancing steps. Then the youngest said:

"Sisters, you all seem to be extra happy tonight but somehow I feel uneasy. I don't know how to explain this but I feel as if some bad luck is coming to us."

"Silly girl," the eldest answered, "something or other seems to scare you all the time. What are you frightened of now? As for this soldier, foolish fellow, he was half asleep even before I gave him our special sleeping-wine. Believe me, he would have slept soundly even without that help."

At last they were all ready and the twelve of them tiptoed to take a look at the soldier. He snored on and did not move hand or foot. Then they closed the door and the eldest led the way back to her own bed. She clapped her hands and at once the bed sank into the floor and a trap-door flew open! The soldier who had got up very quietly when they left him was now peeping through a crack in the door. He saw the twelve of them going down through the trap-door one after the other, the youngest last of all.

As soon as she was out of his sight, the soldier put on his little cloak, opened his door and went across to the trap-door. He found a narrow winding set of stairs below so he carefully walked down and followed the princesses. About half way down the stairs he trod accidentally on the long silk train of the youngest princess. She cried out: "Someone held my dress just now! Oh sisters, I'm scared."

"Silly little girl," the eldest princess said, "you caught it on a nail in the wall," so along they all went again.

Soon they reached the open air outside the castle walls, and they were in an avenue of beautiful trees. The leaves were made of silver which glittered and sparkled and the soldier thought he had better take something to show where they had been. He broke off a little branch and the tree gave a loud crack.

"Did you hear that noise?" the youngest princess cried.

But the eldest said coolly:

"Oh, do stop fussing. It is our princes who are shouting for joy because we are on our way to see them."

They walked on and they came to a row of trees whose leaves were made of gold. Then they went down another avenue where each leaf was a glittering diamond. As the soldier broke off a tiny gold twig and a diamond leaf the trees gave louder and louder cracks. The youngest sister shivered and shook with fear but the eldest sister said:

"The princes are shouting even louder now, that's all."

At last they came to a lake where twelve little boats with a handsome prince in each one, were waiting by the shore. One by one a princess went into each boat and the soldier stepped quietly and carefully into the last boat behind the youngest princess. The princes now rowed over the lake and the prince who was taking the youngest princess across, said: "It is certainly strange but this

boat seems very heavy today. I'm rowing as hard as I can but we are going so slowly and your end of the boat seems lower in the water somehow."

"It must be this warm weather making you feel tired," said the girl. "I feel quite tired as well."

The splendid castle on the other side of the lake was lit by hundreds of torches and candles and the soldier could hear merry music coming from the great hall inside. They got out of the boats and went into the castle and each prince danced with his favourite princess. All this time, the soldier was unseen, so he danced around and between all the dancers. Each time the princesses sat down to take a cup of wine he drank it all up. Their cups were always empty! The youngest girl became frightened again but her sisters told her to enjoy the fun they were having.

They danced until their shoes were worn into holes so at three o'clock in the morning the princes rowed them back across the lake. This time the soldier sat with the eldest princess.

"This boat is so heavy to row," the prince grumbled.

"It is you who are tired," the princess replied.

They reached the shore and the princesses called out:

"Good night, good night! We'll be here tomorrow to dance the night away!"

The soldier ran through the avenues of trees, up the stairs and into his bed. The sisters climbed the stairs wearily for they were tired out with so much dancing. They heard loud snores coming from the soldier's room.

"Our secret is quite safe," they told each other. Then they got undressed, put away their beautiful gowns, pulled off their worn-out slippers and fell fast asleep.

In the morning the soldier got up as though nothing had happened. He thought he would like to watch the wonderful party at the castle over again. So on the second night, the same thing happened as before. The soldier poured away the cup of wine, pretended to fall asleep snoring loudly, and then he followed the princesses – wearing his cloak again, of course.

The third night he did the same – except for one thing. The soldier wanted to make sure that the king would believe his strange story, so when the dancing at the castle was over he carried away, under his cloak, one of the golden wine cups.

On the fourth morning the soldier was ordered to visit the king. He collected his special treasures and off he went. The king was sitting on his throne with his nobles standing nearby – the princesses were hiding behind the door, laughing as they told each other how clever they had been again.

"Where do my twelve daughters dance at night?" asked the king.

"Your Majesty," the soldier bowed low, "they dance with twelve princes in a castle. I know their secret now." He told the king about the sleeping-wine, the trap-door, the lake, the castle, and the princes. The king sent for the princesses.

"Is the soldier's story true?" he demanded and he asked them many questions. Then the soldier brought out the silver, gold and diamond leaves and the golden cup from the castle. The princesses knew that their secret had been discovered at last and they confessed everything to their father.

"I will keep my promise," the king said. "Which princess will you choose for a wife?"

"I'm not very young," replied the soldier, "so I think I will choose the eldest."

They were married that very day and in the end, the poor soldier became first a prince and then a king.

THE NOSE

Three poor soldiers were on their way home after fighting in many battles. One cold dark night they had not found any shelter nearby so they decided to rest in the forest.

"We'd better not all go to sleep at the same time," said one of the soldiers. "There may be some wild beasts in the forest which could attack us." So they decided to take turns at keeping watch. Two of the soldiers curled up in their old coats and fell asleep at once. The third one made their camp-fire blaze brightly and he sat down to keep a look-out. After a while he heard a rustling noise, then a funny little man wearing a bright red jacket appeared.

"Who are you? What are you doing here?" the little man asked.

"I'm just a poor soldier and I'm travelling back from the war. Why don't you warm yourself by the fire. You're very welcome."

"That's very kind of you," said the little man. "Now take this," and he gave the soldier a beautiful red cloak. "Whenever you wear this over your shoulders, you can wish for anything you like." The soldier was very surprised, but before he could say a word, the little man gave a bow and vanished into the forest.

Then it was the second soldier's turn to keep watch. Before long the little man jumped out and asked the soldier all about himself. The soldier asked the little man if he would like to join him by the fire. The little man was very pleased and he handed the second soldier a purse.

"Take care of this," he said as he was leaving, "for it will always remain full of gold no matter how much you take out of it."

Soon it was the third soldier's turn to keep watch. He settled down by the fire and once more, the little man in his red jacket appeared from the trees. The third soldier was just as friendly and polite as the other two.

"Thank you for your kindness," the little man said. "This

horn is my gift to you. Whenever you play it, beautiful music will be heard and crowds of people will gather around to listen and to dance." Then he disappeared.

Before setting off next day the three men talked about the little man and they showed each other their presents. They decided to use the magic purse first of all. They soon had as much gold as they wanted, so they travelled around the world and saw many marvellous sights.

After a while, they grew tired of moving about so much. So the soldier with the red cloak put it over his shoulders and wished for a home for them to share.

"I wish for a castle. It should be strong and tall with lots of towers. I'd like gardens and a lake and, oh yes, horses and a coach with glass windows."

At once all three were standing in front of a fine castle with shining gold turrets. They liked the coach and horses best of all so they decided to use it at once. They drove to the palace of the king who lived nearby. The three of them looked so grand that the king thought they were princes. He welcomed them, then called his beautiful only daughter to meet them. But she was only beautiful to look at. Inside she had the heart of a wicked witch.

They became friends and one day the second soldier was in the palace gardens with this princess and he showed her his wonderful purse. Immediately she wanted it for herself and she planned to steal it somehow. She went to her room and secretly made another purse. It was exactly the same as the soldier's. That night, after much eating and drinking, everybody was very sleepy. The princess stole the magic purse out of the soldier's pocket and she left hers there instead. The next day the three friends returned to their castle. Later on the second soldier opened his purse to get out some gold, but the purse was empty.

"What can have happened?" He was very puzzled, then he remembered something. "The princess was very interested in my purse yesterday. She must have stolen mine when I was asleep after the feast. Then she put this other one in its place. Oh my poor friends, what shall we do without any money?"

"Don't worry," said the first soldier. "I'll get your purse back for you." He flung his magic cloak around him. "I wish to be carried to the princess in the king's palace," he said. In a flash he found the princess. She was piling up gold coins as fast as she could take them out of the purse.

"One thousand, two thousand," she counted greedily, then she noticed the soldier.

"Help! Thieves! Help! Robbers!" she screamed.

The soldier was frightened for servants and guards came running when they heard the screams. He knew nobody would believe his story so he ran to the window and jumped out. He forgot all about using his magic cloak. Unluckily, it got caught on the thorns in the rose bushes. He dared not stop to pull it away so he had to leave it behind as he climbed over the garden wall. The witch-princess was delighted when she saw this because she knew the wonderful things that the cloak could do.

The first soldier trudged wearily back to the castle. He felt very sad, so the third soldier took out the horn which the little man had given to him. He played some jolly tunes to cheer his friend up and as soon as he did this, crowds of people gathered in the castle gardens to hear the happy music.

"I have an idea," the first soldier said. "Let us ask everybody to get into a long line and we will lead these people to the palace. Then we'll make that wicked princess give you back the purse and the red cloak."

They thought this was a good idea so the third soldier went on playing and everybody trooped off to the palace.

The princess saw what was happening so she quickly took off her fine dress and put on an old ragged one. She put some pins, needles and ribbons in a basket. Then she and her maid slipped quietly out of the palace and joined the crowds. The princess walked around, pretending to be a poor girl selling little things from her basket. When everybody was having supper, she started to sing a magic song. This put a wicked spell upon the crowds. It made them stop whatever they were doing. The three soldiers stood perfectly still as though they were on guard. Then her maid slipped up to the third soldier and stole his horn. The princess stopped singing and they both ran back to the palace. The three soldiers now had nothing – except the castle! No cloak, no purse and no horn!

"What shall we do now?" asked the first soldier. "We'd better make some plans very carefully."

So they sat down and they thought and they thought. But after a time the second soldier said sadly, "Dear old friends, perhaps it would be better if we went off by ourselves. We must seek out our own future." The others agreed so they shook hands and they parted.

Two of them decided that they would travel together for a time, but the second soldier went off by himself. He walked until he was very tired and hungry. To his surprise, he noticed that he was in the very same wood where he and his friends had met the little man in his bright red coat. It was growing dark, so he lay down under a tree to sleep.

The next day bright warm sunshine woke him up and as he was stretching and yawning he noticed that the branches above him were covered with rosy-red apples. He was hungry so he picked and ate one. Then he ate another and then a third. But his nose started to feel very odd. He touched it and it seemed to be growing longer, and longer, and longer. Soon his nose reached the ground and it just went on growing. It curled itself in and out and around the trees until it stretched to the edge of the wood. The poor man sat under the apple tree, feeling very worried indeed.

In the meantime his two soldier friends were travelling along when they spotted something lying across their path.

"Whatever is this?" the first one said.

"Please don't think I am being stupid," the third soldier said, "but I think er – er – I think it is a *nose*!"

"A nose! Why bless my soul you are right. Whoever heard of a

nose on a path? Shall we follow it and see who is the owner of this wonderful enormous nose?"

They walked through the woods and they had a great shock when they found their old friend at the end of the nose, quite unable to move. They tried to lift him up but he was far too heavy. The three old friends sat together wondering what to do when suddenly the little man with the red coat appeared.

"I'll help you," he said. "Pick a pear from that pear tree and take a bite," he said to the first soldier. The soldier did as he was told. At once his nose went back to its proper size.

"Now listen carefully," the little man went on, "just pick a few of these apples and take them to the princess. Ask her to taste the best apples in the world." With these words, he vanished.

The second soldier dressed himself in gardener's clothes and went to the palace. He said he had a very special present for the princess, so the maid took him straight to her mistress.

The apples looked so ripe and rosy that the princess was soon munching away. She ate one and was biting a second when her nose started growing longer and longer. Soon it went out of the window and around the gardens.

The king was extremely upset. "My daughter is very ill," he announced. "I'll give a big reward to anyone who can make her better."

The soldier took off the gardener's clothes and now he dressed like a very important doctor.

"Show me to the princess's room for I alone can cure her," he said. He asked for a knife and he chopped an apple into small pieces.

"Take a few pieces twice a day," he ordered, "and I'll call again tomorrow." He knew her nose would grow longer and longer but he wanted to punish her for stealing his purse.

Next day the princess was crying and shouting that her nose was even longer! The 'doctor' left her some pieces of magic pear for her to eat this time.

"My nose is a little smaller," the princess said crossly the next day, "but I don't think you are a very good doctor if you can't make me better at once."

"I can see you are still a rude princess," the soldier thought.

126

"Take this chopped apple for one more day," he said aloud, "and I'll call again tomorrow."

Well, the princess's nose grew longer and longer.

"It's getting worse, you stupid doctor!" she cried the next day. "Your medicine is useless."

"No," said the soldier in a fierce voice, "do not blame my medicine. It is you who are to blame. I know that you have stolen three things. Unless you hand them back, your nose will never get better."

"What nonsense," the princess shouted angrily, "I've never stolen anything!"

"Very well," said the soldier, "I'll have to tell the king all about this now."

The king listened carefully to the 'doctor's' words.

"I order you to return this cloak, purse and horn or you will leave the palace for ever," the king told his daughter angrily.

So the princess returned all three things to the 'doctor'. When he was sure that they were quite safe, he made her eat a whole magic pear. At once her nose returned to its proper size. As for the three soldiers, they took great care of the cloak, the purse and the horn and they lived happily in their castle from that day on.

THE BAKER'S CAT

Once there was an old lady, Mrs Jones, who lived with her cat, Mog. Mrs Jones kept a baker's shop, in a little tiny town, at the bottom of a valley between two mountains.

Every morning you could see Mrs Jones's light twinkle on, long before all the other houses in the town, because she got up very early to bake loaves and buns and jam tarts and Welsh cakes.

First thing in the morning Mrs Jones lit a big fire. Then she made dough, out of flour and water and sugar and yeast. Then she put the dough into pans and set it in front of the fire to rise.

Mog got up early too. He got up to catch mice. When he had chased all the mice out of the bakery, he wanted to sit in front of the warm fire. But Mrs Jones wouldn't let him, because of the loaves and buns there, rising in their pans.

She said, "Don't sit on the buns, Mog."

The buns were rising nicely. They were getting fine and big. That is what yeast does. It makes bread and buns and cakes swell up and get bigger and bigger.

As Mog was not allowed to sit by the fire, he went to play in the sink.

Most cats hate water, but Mog didn't. He loved it. He liked to sit by the tap, hitting the drops with his paw as they fell, and getting water all over his whiskers!

What did Mog look like? His back, and his sides, and his legs down as far as where his socks would have come to, and his face and ears and his tail were all marmalade coloured.

His stomach and his waistcoat and his paws were white. And he had a white tassel at the tip of his tail, white fringes to his ears, and white whiskers.

The water made his marmalade fur go almost fox colour and his paws and waistcoat shining-white clean.

But Mrs Jones said, "Mog, you are getting too excited. You are shaking water all over my pans of buns, just when they are getting nice and big. Run along and play outside."

Mog was affronted. He put his ears and tail down (when cats are pleased they put their ears and tails up) and he went out. It was raining hard.

A rushing rocky river ran through the middle of the town. Mog went and sat in the water and looked for fish. But there were no fish in that part of the river. Mog got wetter and wetter. But he didn't care. Presently he began to sneeze.

Then Mrs Jones opened her door and called, "Mog! I have put the buns in the oven. You can come in now, and sit by the fire."

Mog was so wet that he was shiny all over, as if he had been polished. As he sat by the fire he sneezed nine times.

Mrs Jones said, "Oh dear, my poor Mog, are you catching a cold?"

She dried him with a towel and gave him some warm milk with yeast in it. Yeast is good for people when they are poorly.

Then she left him sitting in front of the fire and began making jam tarts. When she had put the tarts in the oven she went out shopping, taking her umbrella.

But what do you think was happening to Mog?

The yeast was making him rise.

As he sat dozing in front of the lovely warm fire he was growing bigger and bigger.

First he grew as big as a sheep.

Then he grew as big as a donkey.

Then he grew as big as a cart-horse.

Then he grew as big as a hippopotamus.

By now he was too big for Mrs Jones's little kitchen, but he was far too big to get through the door. He just burst the walls.

When Mrs Jones came home with her shopping-bag and her umbrella she cried out,

"Mercy me, what is happening to my house?"

The whole house was bulging. It was swaying. Huge whiskers were poking out of the kitchen window. A marmalade-coloured paw came out of one bedroom window, and an ear with a white fringe out of the other.

"Morow?" said Mog. He was waking up from his nap and trying to stretch.

Then the whole house fell down.

"Oh, Mog!" cried Mrs Jones. "Look what you've done."

The people in the town were astonished when they saw what had happened. They could hardly believe their eyes.

They gave Mrs Jones the Town Hall to live in, because they were so fond of her (and her buns). But they were not so sure about Mog.

The Mayor said, "Suppose he goes on growing and breaks our Town Hall? Suppose he turns fierce? It would not be safe to have him in the town, he is too big."

Mrs Jones said, "Mog is a gentle cat. He would not hurt anybody."

"We will wait and see about that," said the Mayor. "Suppose he sat down on someone? Suppose he was hungry? What will he eat? He had better live outside the town, up on the mountain."

So everybody shouted, "Shoo! Scram! Pssst! Shoo!" and poor Mog was driven outside the town gates. It was still raining hard. Water was rushing down the mountains. Not that Mog cared.

But poor Mrs Jones was very sad. She began making a new lot of loaves and buns in the Town Hall, crying into them so much that the dough was too wet, and very salty.

Mog walked up the valley between the two mountains. By now he was bigger than an elephant – almost as big as a whale! When the sheep on the mountain saw him coming, they were scared to death and galloped away. But he took no notice of them. He was looking for fish in the river. He caught lots of fish! He was having a fine time.

By now it had been raining for so long that Mog heard a loud, watery roar at the top of the valley. He saw a huge wall of water coming towards him. The river was beginning to flood, as more and more rain-water poured down into it, off the mountains.

Mog thought, "If I don't stop that water, all these fine fish will be washed away."

So he sat down, plump in the middle of the valley, and he spread himself out like a big, fat cottage loaf.

The water could not get by.

The people in the town had heard the roar of the flood-water. They were very frightened. The Mayor shouted, "Run up the mountains before the water gets to the town, or we shall all be drowned!"

So they all rushed up the mountains, some on one side of the town, some on the other.

What did they see then?

Why, Mog, sitting in the middle of the valley. Beyond him was a great lake.

"Mrs Jones," said the Mayor, "can you make your cat stay there till we have built a dam across the valley, to keep all that water back?"

"I will try," said Mrs Jones. "He mostly sits still if he is tickled under his chin."

So for three days everybody in the town took turns tickling Mog under his chin with hay-rakes. He purred and purred and purred. His purring made big waves roll right across the lake of flood-water.

All this time the best builders were making a great dam across the valley.

People brought Mog all sorts of nice things to eat, too – bowls of cream and condensed milk, liver and bacon, sardines, even chocolate! But he was not hungry. He had eaten so much fish.

On the third day they finished the dam. The town was safe.

The Mayor said, "I can see now that Mog is a gentle cat. He can live in the Town Hall with you, Mrs Jones. Here is a badge for him to wear."

The badge was on a silver chain to go round his neck. It said MOG SAVED OUR TOWN.

So Mrs Jones and Mog lived happily ever after in the Town Hall. If you should go to the little town of Carnmog you may see the policeman holding up the traffic while Mog walks through the streets on his way to catch fish in the lake for breakfast. His tail waves above the houses and his whiskers rattle against the upstairs windows. But people know he will not hurt them, because he is a gentle cat.

He loves to play in the lake and sometimes he gets so wet that he sneezes. But Mrs Jones is not going to give him any more yeast.

He is quite big enough already!

THE BRAVE LITTLE TAILOR

A little tailor once thought to himself:
"Ho hum, it's a lovely summer day. I'd like to have an adventure. What shall I take with me?"

He could only find some cheese. As that was better than nothing he popped it into his bag, together with his fiddle. He shut his front door and his old hen came squawking by, so he packed her in as well! Then he set off.

He climbed to the top of a hill and there he met a giant.

"Good morning, friend," he said. "I see you are looking at the whole wide world. I'm looking for adventures. Would you like to come with me?"

"What! Go with a funny little fellow like you?" and the giant laughed.

"I may be little," said the tailor, "but I am the better man."

"Ho, ho!" said the giant, "we'll soon see who is the master." And he picked up a stone. He squeezed it until a few drops of water came out. "If you are strong, try and do that."

"Is that all?" said the tailor. "Just watch me then." And he took the cheese from his bag. He squeezed, and plenty of whey dripped onto the ground. "What do you think of that?" asked the tailor cheekily. "My squeeze was much better than yours."

The giant did not notice that it was a cheese so he had nothing to say. Then he picked up another stone and he threw it so high that it almost vanished.

"Beat that, little fellow, if you can."

"Yes, it was quite a good throw," the tailor agreed, "but your stone fell back here. I'll throw something that will not fall at all."

"You'll never do that!" the giant roared.

The tailor lifted the old hen out of his bag and tossed her into the air. She was so pleased to be free that she flew out of sight.

"What do you think about that then?"

"You are a clever little fellow," the giant said, "but I'd like to see what work you can do."

He took him into the forest and showed him a fine big oak tree which he had cut down.

"Shall we pull this down the hill together?"

"Certainly, giant. You had better carry the thick trunk and I'll carry the leaves and branches.

The giant heaved the trunk over his shoulders but the cunning little man quietly sat back very comfortably on a leafy branch. He let the giant carry the tree trunk, the branches and himself! He sang and whistled merry little tunes as though carrying trees was the easiest thing in the world. The giant struggled on but at last he stopped. "I must have a rest," he said. The tailor jumped down quickly. He held the tree as if he had been carrying it. "I'm surprised that a giant like you cannot carry this oak tree," he said.

After a short rest, they went on until they came to a cherry tree. The giant pulled down the top branch and picked some juicy cherries. Then he handed it to his little friend. Of course the tailor could not hold the branch down and he went swinging high into the air.

"What's this," the giant called. "Can't you hold a small branch down?"

"Of course I can but I can see a hunter with a gun. He is aiming at the bush where you are standing now. I jumped over the tree to get out of his way. Why don't you do the same?"

The giant tried hard to do this but the tree was too high for him to jump over.

"Well," the giant said, "you are a good little fellow. Why don't you rest at my house tonight with a friend of mine?"

"That is kind of you, giant. I am a little tired."

So off they went together. There was another giant waiting for them and they had a good supper. The giant showed his little friend to a comfortable bed and they said 'Good night' to each other. But the tailor thought the giant was up to something and as soon as he had left the room the tailor jumped out of bed, curled up in a corner and went straight to sleep.

As the clock struck midnight, the giant came creeping softly in carrying an iron bar. He did not stop to look closely at the bed

but hit it with a tremendous blow.

"That has finished you off, my little grasshopper," he muttered. "I shan't have any more trouble from you."

In the morning the two giants went off to the forest as usual. They heard someone whistling a happy tune. It was the little tailor! They had forgotten all about him. They were so amazed, and then frightened, that they turned round and ran away just as fast as ever they could.

Meanwhile the tailor wandered on until he arrived at the king's palace.

"Does the king need a strong fellow to serve him? I am very clever and I know how to trick wicked people very easily," he boasted. People all around began to laugh at such fine words coming from this small fellow. But the king sent for him and said: "Two wicked giants live in the forest not far away. They rob the people and steal their cows and sometimes they set fire to houses. If you are as clever as you say you are, will you get rid of them for me? If you win, I will give you half my kingdom."

"I'll be glad to help, your majesty," he said.

So, he marched off to the edge of the forest. He was very careful and his sharp eyes looked to the left and to the right. Before

long he heard a funny rumbling noise. He crept along and spotted the giants fast asleep under a tree. Their snoring was making the branches of the tree wave up and down.

"I've got them now," the tailor thought. He filled his pockets with stones, some large and some small. Then he climbed the tree and made himself comfortable on a branch hidden in the leaves. He let a few small stones drop on to the chest of the first giant. He moved and grunted in his sleep and went on snoring. But when a few more stones hit him he gave the second giant a hard push.

"Stop hitting me on my chest," he said.

"No one has touched you, silly," the second giant said sleepily. "You've been dreaming."

They muttered and grumbled and went back to sleep. The tailor threw some middle-sized stones, on the second giant's chest this time.

"What do you think you're doing? Do stop it. That hurt me," he said. The other giant yawned. "Stop doing what?"

"Stop hitting me, you have really hurt me," and he rubbed his chest. They grumbled and pushed each other a bit and then they closed their eyes.

This time the little tailor picked out the biggest stone of all. He

threw it as hard as he could, right in the middle of the first giant's chest.

"You've gone too far this time!" he shouted. He jumped up and he began to hit the other giant with his enormous fists. He sprang to his feet to defend himself and a dreadful battle began. They hit each other with rocks. In the end they hit each other so hard that they fell senseless to the ground.

The tailor jumped down from his branch and finished off the two giants with his little sword.

He returned to the king. "It is all over," he announced. "The giants used stones to defend themselves. But it was no use. It was hard work but the giants are dead now." The tailor asked for his reward.

"You have done very well," the king said, "but there is one more thing I should like you to do."

"What is it?" asked the tailor.

"In a cellar in the palace there is a bear. If you can spend a night alone with it, you shall have your reward at once." He thought he'd get rid of the tailor in this way, for no one had ever escaped alive from the bear's sharp claws.

"That sounds easy to me," was the tailor's reply.

So that evening he was taken to the cellar and the door was locked. He shook the bear's paw and they promised to be friends then he took some walnuts out of his pockets. He cracked them with his teeth and nibbled the inside.

"Would you like to try some?" he asked the bear, but he handed him some small brown pebbles instead of walnuts. The bear tried but he could not open them.

"Aren't your teeth strong enough? Here, let me show you."

Again, the tailor put a walnut in his mouth and cracked it open.

"I'm sure I can do that, now that I've watched you," the bear growled. He took the stones again and bit with all his strength until he broke every single tooth. This made him so tired that he had to lie down for a rest.

The tailor did not think the bear would sleep very long so he pulled out the fiddle from his bag and he played a happy tune. The bear liked this and he started to dance around on his back legs.

"I'd like to make music too. Is it hard to play a fiddle?"

"Oh no, it's quite easy. You hold it in your left hand, like this. Then you take this long bow in your right hand and pull it over the strings. That's all there is to do."

"Will you teach me some tunes? Then I can have music whenever I feel like dancing."

"Most certainly. But, oh dear, your claws are so long. They'll get in the way, so first I'll sew them down."

The bear lifted his paws and the tailor whipped out a needle and sewed them down very tight.

"I'll teach you the fiddle tomorrow," he said and he curled up on the bear's straw and went to sleep. The bear growled but without teeth and claws he could do nothing so he slept as well.

In the morning the king found the tailor and the bear chatting happily.

"You truly deserve your reward," he said and he gave half his kingdom to the brave little tailor. Some people say he was a clever little tailor as well.

THE SWINEHERD

In a small country long ago there lived a poor prince. He was in love with the daughter of a rich emperor. He had no riches to give her, but he did have a very special rose bush that grew in his garden. It only ever had one flower at a time and this one bloomed every five years. But it was a very beautiful rose. It smelt so sweet that as soon as you smelt it you forgot all your troubles and worries. And this day the rose was in flower. So the prince dug up the bush to give to the princess.

Then he called to his pet nightingale. This little bird could sing every song in the world. He told his servant to carry the two presents to the emperor's palace.

"How pretty!" said the court ladies when they saw the rose.

"It is charming," said the emperor.

The princess touched it and she almost cried. "But father, how horrid!" she said. "It is a real rose! It isn't made of silk!"

"Ugh, a real rose," the court ladies then said.

"Let us look at the other present," the emperor said soothingly. The nightingale sang so beautifully that at first nobody could say anything unpleasant about it.

"It is a proper little nightingale," said the servant holding the cage.

"Then let it fly away," said the princess rudely. "You can tell the prince I do not like his presents and he need not come to visit me."

This did not seem to worry the prince. He put on some old clothes and pulled a hat right down over his eyes. Then he went boldly along to visit the emperor.

"Good day," he said. "Do you have any work I could do for you?"

"At present I need someone to look after the royal pigs but nobody ever wants that job."

"Oh but I do! I'll take it." So the prince was made the

140

emperor's swineherd. He now lived in a tiny room near the pigsties. He looked after the pigs and in his spare time he made a pretty little pot with bells all around the top. When the pot boiled, a pretty tune rang out. But there was something else it could do. When the royal swineherd held his finger over the boiling pot he knew at once what was cooking in every kitchen in the land.

The princess was out walking with her maid of honour when she heard the little bells.

"I know that tune," she said. "I can play it on my piano." She saw the little pot bubbling away on the fire. "I'd like to have that pot. Go and ask the swineherd how much it costs."

The maid went close to the pigsties.

"How much do you want for that pot?" she inquired.

"I want ten kisses from the princess," the swineherd said.

"Oh my goodness!" The maid ran back to her mistress.

"What did he say?"

"I don't like to say it aloud."

"Well, whisper it." So the maid whispered to the princess.

"Impossible! He is very rude. I do want that pot though! Ask him if he'll take ten kisses, from my maids of honour."

"I'm afraid not," came the reply. "It's ten kisses from the princess or she doesn't get the pot!"

"Bother! Well, you must all stand round me so that nobody sees me."

The maids of honour spread out their lovely dresses: the swineherd had his ten kisses and the princess had her pot.

They went back to the palace and the pot was kept boiling all that day. "We know what everybody is having for dinner," they told each other. "Turtle soup, lamb cutlets, rabbit stew, figgy pudding, apple pie, and pancakes! We can smell them all." It was great fun indeed.

The royal swineherd looked after the pigs very well but he was always making something or other. One day he made a wooden rattle. When he swung this round his head, it played every dance in the world – waltzes, polkas and square dances and many more.

"That is wonderful," the princess said when she heard it playing. "Go and find out how much it costs. But I won't give any more kisses!"

Her maid of honour went down to the pigsty.

"He demands one hundred kisses," she said when she returned.

"That is impossible. The swineherd must be mad," and the princess stamped her foot. She walked away but then she stopped.

"I am the emperor's daughter," she said, "I must possess beautiful things like that rattle. So go and tell him I'll give him ten kisses like the last time. He can take ninety from my maids of honour."

So the maid of honour went back but she returned with the same message: "One hundred kisses from the princess or he keeps the rattle."

"I suppose I must agree, you must stand all round me though," she ordered. So the maids of honour spread out their skirts and the swineherd kissed the princess.

Just then the emperor was walking towards the pigsties. "What's going on?" he said and he stood on tiptoe. Nobody noticed him for the maids of honour were too busy counting: "eighty-two, eighty-three . . ." The swineherd was taking the eighty-sixth kiss when the emperor took off his golden slipper and hit them all on the head.

"What is going on here? Who is kissing my daughter? Why, it is the swineherd!"

The emperor was extremely angry.

"I banish you from my kingdom," he said to his daughter. "You must leave at once."

The princess stood there and cried bitterly.

"Oh how unhappy I am! I wish I had welcomed the handsome prince when he came. How silly I have been." Then the swineherd washed his face, took off his ragged clothes, and put on his prince's robes. He looked so fine and handsome that the princess curtsied at once.

"You threw away the lovely rose and the sweet singing nightingale but for a cooking pot and a baby's rattle you kissed a swineherd. Well, losing a kingdom is your reward!"

He turned away and went back to his own little kingdom where he married a princess who looked after the rose and the nightingale very well indeed.

THE PIED PIPER OF HAMELIN

In the north of Germany there is a town called Hamelin, near Brunswick. It is a pretty place with flowers and trees everywhere. But long ago, hundreds and thousands of rats thought that they would like to live there. What a terrible time then began for the people of Hamelin. The rats gobbled up food, they scampered through the kitchens and went to the bedrooms. Here they jumped onto the beds and burrowed under the blankets. Nobody wanted to share a bed with a dozen rats!

> *'They fought the dogs and killed the cats,*
> *And bit the babies in their cradles,*
> *And ate the cheeses out of the vats,*
> *And licked the soup from the cooks' own ladles,*
> *Made nests inside men's Sunday hats,*
> *And even spoiled the women's chats*
> *By drowning their speaking*
> *With shrieking and squeaking*
> *In fifty different sharps and flats!'*

Soon every scrap of food disappeared. The rats had eaten everything and had started to chew and gnaw at the wooden tables and chairs. By now the townspeople were hungry and they were very angry. They marched along to the town hall in the market place and they demanded to see the mayor.

The mayor quaked in his shoes as he came outside.

"Good people," he said. His voice quivered. "It is such a pity that these rats have come to Hamelin . . ."

"A pity!" people shouted. "Is that all you can say? We want you to do something about them and we want you to do it now!"

The mayor wrung his hands for he did not know what to say. Then he had an idea. He went inside and came back with a large bag. "This bag of gold will be given as a reward to anyone who

143

can clear our town of rats," and he held it up for everyone to see. A lot of noise went on as the crowd talked about the mayor's plan. Suddenly they heard a loud shout.

"I'll get rid of all the rats from this town for you!"

There was silence as people turned their heads around to try and see who was speaking. It was a young man but he was a stranger to them all. He was wearing a wonderful coat! One half of it was yellow and the other was red. On his head he was wearing a bright green pointed cap with a long feather hanging down from the top. Around his neck there was a thick red and yellow cord with a musical pipe tied at the end of it. His trousers were as green as grass and he wore one red pointed shoe and one yellow one.

"They call me the Pied Piper," he said.

His clothes were so strange that people laughed and joked unkindly as he moved forward to the bottom of the steps.

"If I can take away every single rat from Hamelin, will you give me that bag of gold?" he asked.

The mayor would have promised anything at all but he replied:

"I give you my promise and we will always be thankful to you."

All the people and the children agreed with their mayor and they watched closely as the Pied Piper untied the pipe from around his neck. He put it to his lips and took a deep breath. Then he blew a long silvery note, then another and another. The townspeople could not believe their eyes for this is what happened!

'And ere three shrill notes the pipe uttered,
You heard as if an army muttered;
And the muttering grew to a mighty rumbling,
And out of the houses the rats came tumbling.
Great rats, small rats, lean rats, brawny rats,
Brown rats, black rats, grey rats, tawny rats,
Fathers, mothers, uncles, cousins
Families by tens and dozens,
Brothers, sisters, husbands, wives –
Followed the Piper for their lives.'

The Piper with the long feather streaming out behind him, moved across the market square and the rats moved with him. The mayor and his friends rushed to open wide the big gates of the

town and the rats poured through like a flood. There were thousands and thousands of them, far too many to count, and they ran along the country roads in a long procession. The Pied Piper marched in front of them but he never stopped playing the special tune on his pipe.

They ran and ran until they came to a valley between the hills. A special cheese was standing there, the biggest that had ever been made. It had thousands of holes in it and the rats scurried inside. Soon the very last rat disappeared with a twitch of its tail and the holes in the cheese closed up, never to open again.

The Piper turned around and went happily back to Hamelin. He was in a hurry to collect his reward. All the townsfolk were watching from the town walls and as soon as they saw him returning without the rats, they started to cheer. "No more rats!" they shouted and they rushed to shake his hand. The Pied Piper went on to the town hall. "Your rats have gone for ever," he said. "I've come for the reward you promised me."

But the mayor became grumpy and greedy.

"This young man is only a strange wanderer," he muttered, "why should we give him this big bag of gold? He only piped a tune and went for a little walk in the country."

He picked one gold coin out of the bag and threw it at the Pied Piper's feet. "That should be payment enough for your tune," he said rudely. The people all around nodded their heads. They were as mean as the mayor! They had forgotten already the wonderful thing the Piper had done for them.

The young man looked at them in silence. Then he frowned.

"The mayor has broken his promise. These people are just as bad," he thought. "How ungrateful as well as dishonest! And I'm afraid their children may learn these wicked ways from them. I must do something to help them, I think."

He walked to the town gates but he still did not say a word to anyone. At the gate, he slowly untied his pipe. The crowds stopped their jeers and shouts and began to look worried and uneasy. The Piper took a deep breath and he blew three long silvery notes. Then he played many happy joyful tunes and he started to dance. He waved his arm and he invited all the children to dance as well. First the children in the market place ran to him.

Then doors opened in every house and out of them poured children of every age, even babies just learning to toddle. They ran along the streets to the gate and the Pied Piper went on playing his merry tunes.

> '*Out came the children running*
> *All the little boys and girls,*
> *With rosy cheeks and flaxen curls,*
> *And sparkling eyes and teeth like pearls,*
> *Tripping and skipping, ran merrily after*
> *The wonderful music with shouting and laughter.*'

The mayor and the men and women stood like statues made of stone as the town gate swung open. The children laughed as they followed the piper. They joined hands in a long chain and danced away into the countryside.

The Piper went on playing his pipe and the children did not look back at the town of Hamelin but they sang and danced their way right over the highest hills, across the River Weser, to a faraway land where people were kind and welcoming to strangers and always kept their promises.

THE GIRAFFE
WHO SAW TO THE END
OF THE WORLD

In a jungle that was almost a forest, and in a forest that was almost a wood, and in a wood that was almost a garden, there once lived an elephant and a flower and a pig and a giraffe and a kuputte-bird. There was also a hyena there and a plinkinplonk and monkeys as well; and of course there was a forest of moonbeams, and a silver ant that dreamt of silence, and a river that told the strangest stories.

Sometimes the giraffe came to the hill where the elephant and the flower lived. The giraffe had a very long neck, and when it stood on top of the hill and stretched its neck it could see over the trees and mountains to the end of the world.

One day the flower asked, "What is the end of the world like?"

"Beautiful," said the giraffe.

"What lives there?" asked the elephant.

"Giraffes, of course," answered the giraffe.

The elephant had always thought elephants lived at the end of the world. And the flower had always thought only flowers could live in such a faraway place.

"Isn't there even one elephant there?" asked the elephant.

The giraffe stretched its neck as hard as it could. It looked across the trees and the mountains for a long time, and then said, "No, only giraffes."

"Maybe the giraffes are hiding a few flowers," suggested the flower.

"Most certainly not," said the giraffe.

"He's not telling the truth," said a voice above them. It was the sparrow, who had been sitting all the time on the giraffe's head. "I can see the end of the world a little better than he can, and it's full of sparrows. Very large sparrows, even larger than eagles."

The giraffe said it had forgotten to mention sparrows, as they were smaller than giraffes.

"But there are quite definitely no elephants or flowers there," the giraffe insisted.

"You're quite right," agreed the sparrow.

The elephant and the flower decided to go for a walk instead of listening to the other two creatures, who were now boasting loudly. On their walk they asked all the creatures they met, "What do you think lives at the end of the world?" And the ant-eater said ant-eaters, and the snake said snakes, and the pig said pigs and the lizard said lizards. And every single creature thought the only things that lived at the end of the world were just like themselves, only a little larger.

Later in the afternoon when the elephant and the flower returned to the hill, they found all the creatures they had met on their walk gathered round the giraffe. The giraffe and the sparrow had agreed that only giraffes and sparrows lived at the end of the world. They were telling the other creatures that there were lakes and forests and rivers and trees and even weeds there. But no other animals.

The animals were very indignant. "We want to see for ourselves," they shouted.

"You can't," said the giraffe. "You're not tall enough."

"You can't," said the sparrow. "You've got no wings."

Then the pig had one of its rare ideas. "We'll all climb up the giraffe's neck and see for ourselves," it said.

The giraffe didn't like the idea, especially as it was the pig's.

"It's a stupid idea," it said. "Fancy a pig trying to make a suggestion of any kind. It's bound to fail."

But the other animals did not agree. They wanted to see the end of the world for themselves and they shouted and grunted so much that the giraffe had to agree to the pig's idea.

So first the snake climbed up. "Just as I thought," it said. "The end of the world is full of snakes."

"Nonsense," squeaked the pig, and he began to climb up the giraffe, slipping every now and then. He clung to the giraffe's ears and shouted down: "The snake's lying as usual. The end of the world's full of pigs. Very beautiful pigs. I can even see a King Pig sitting on a throne."

"Rubbish," shouted the ant-eater. "Let's have a look."

And when the ant-eater had reached the top it said, "Why what glorious ant-eaters there are! And so many ants to eat as well."

"I still think that they're all wrong," said the sparrow who was fluttering above the ant-eater. "I'm the furthest up, and so have the clearest view. It's definitely sparrows."

And so the creatures began to argue.

"High up is far enough up to see the end of the world," they shouted at the sparrow. And the pig was so angry it nearly fell down.

"Take your feet out of my ears," it squeaked at the ant-eater, who was sitting unsteadily on top of it. "And take your hoof off my head," shouted the snake.

As they argued, other creatures began to climb up the giraffe's neck. For miles and miles around, the jungle was full of talk and speculation about what lived at the end of the world.

Soon there was a gigantic pile of creatures on top of the giraffe's head. There were snakes and ant-eaters and pigs and frogs and monkeys and the white rabbit as well. Only the larger jungle creatures stayed on the ground with the elephant and the flower. They thought it a rather undignified heap, and knew quite well what lived at the end of the world.

The giraffe's neck was beginning to ache and strain.

All the time the creatures had been clambering over each other, a caterpillar had been slowly working its way up the giraffe's neck. It climbed on to the pig's head and stood upright. It was a very timid caterpillar and was a bit afraid of saying that the world was full of caterpillars. But it didn't have to anyway. The weight of all the creatures had become too much for the giraffe. It staggered on its feet, then tumbled down the hill. The creatures fell down on top of it in a huge heap. They all wriggled and groaned. And when they had untangled themselves they surrounded the caterpillar.

"It's your fault," said the pig. "It was your weight that made us fall. Now you'll have to settle the argument."

The caterpillar was very afraid of the animals, and it didn't want to make them any angrier by saying the end of the world was full of caterpillars.

So it said: "The end of the world's full of everything."

Though the other creatures did not believe it, they were so relieved that it wasn't full of caterpillars they agreed that maybe the caterpillar could see best after all. And so they went home happy, leaving the flower and the elephant alone on the hill. It was getting dark anyway.

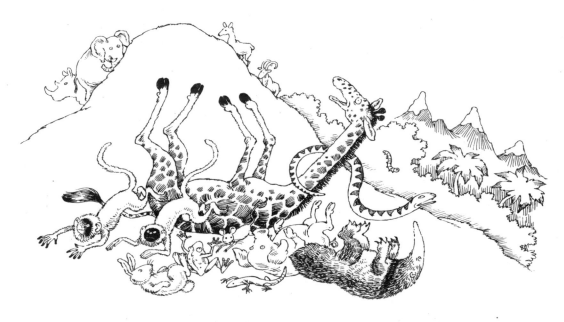

THE FAIRY SHIP

Little Tom was the son of a sailor. He lived in a small white-washed cottage in Cornwall, on the rocky cliffs looking over the sea. From his bedroom window he could watch the great waves with their curling plumes of white foam, and count the seagulls as they circled in the blue sky. Tom's father was somewhere out on that great stretch of ocean, and all Tom's thoughts were there, following him, wishing for him to come home. Every day he ran down the narrow path to the small rocky bay, and sat there waiting for the ship to return.

December brought wild winds that swept the coast. Little Tom was kept indoors, for the gales would have blown him away like a gull's feather if he had gone to the rocky pathway. He was deeply disappointed that he couldn't keep watch in his favourite place. A letter had come, saying that his father was on his way home and any time he might arrive. Tom feared he wouldn't be there to see him, and he stood by the window for hours watching the sky and the wild tossing sea.

"What shall I have for Christmas, Mother?" he asked one day. "Will Father Christmas remember to bring me something?"

"Perhaps he will, if our ship comes home in time," smiled his mother, and then she sighed and looked out at the wintry scene.

"Will he come in a sleigh with eight reindeer pulling it?" persisted Tom.

"Maybe he will," said his mother, but she wasn't thinking what she was saying. Tom knew at once, and he pulled her skirt.

"Father Christmas won't come in a sleigh, because there isn't any snow here. Besides, it is too rocky, and the reindeer would slip. I think he'll come in a ship, a grand ship with blue sails and a gold mast."

Tom's mother suddenly laughed aloud.

"Of course he will, little Tom. Father Christmas comes in a sleigh drawn by a team of reindeer to the children of towns and

152

villages, but to the children of the sea he sails in a ship with all the presents tucked away in the hold."

She took her little son up in her arms and kissed him, but he struggled away and went back to the window.

Christmas morning came, and it was a day of surprising sunshine and calm. The seas danced into the cove in sparkling waves, and fluttered their flags of white foam, and tossed their treasures of seaweed and shells on the narrow beach.

Tom's mother's face was happy and excited, as if she had a secret. Her eyes shone with joy, and she seemed to dance round the room in excitement, but she said nothing.

Tom ate his breakfast quietly – a bantam egg and some honey for a special treat. Then he ran outside, to the gate, and down the slippery grassy path which led to the sea.

"Where are you going, Tom?" called his mother. "You wait here, and you'll see something."

"No, Mother. I'm going to look for the ship, the little Christmas ship," he answered, and away he trotted.

The water was deep blue, like the sky, and purple shadows hovered over it, as the waves gently rocked the cormorants fishing there. The little boy leaned back in his sheltered spot, and the sound of the water made him drowsy. The sweet air lulled him and his head began to droop.

Then he saw a sight so beautiful he had to rub his eyes to get the sleep out of them. The wintry sun made a pathway on the water, flickering with points of light on the crests of the waves, and down this golden lane came a tiny ship that seemed no larger than a toy. She moved swiftly through the water, making for the cove, and Tom cried out with joy and clapped his hands as she approached.

The wind filled the blue satin sails, and the sunbeams caught the mast of gold. On deck was a company of sailors dressed in white, and they were making music of some kind, for shrill squeaks and whistles and pipings came through the air. Tom leaned forward to watch them, and as the ship came nearer he could see that the little sailors were playing flutes, tootling a hornpipe, then whistling a carol.

He stared very hard at their pointed faces, and little pink ears.

They were not sailor-men at all, but a crew of white mice! There were four-and-twenty of them – yes, twenty-four white mice with gold rings round their snowy necks, and gold rings in their ears!

The little ship sailed into the cove, through the barriers of sharp rocks, and the white mice hurried backward and forward, hauling at the silken ropes, casting the gold anchor, crying with high voices as the ship came to port close to the rock where Tom sat waiting and watching.

Out came the captain – and would you believe it? He was a duck, with a cocked hat and a blue jacket trimmed with gold braid. Tom knew at once he was Captain Duck because under his wing he carried a brass telescope, and by his side was a tiny sword.

"Quack! Quack!" said the captain, saluting Tom, and Tom of course stood up and saluted back.

"The ship's cargo is ready, Sir," said the duck. "We have sailed across the sea to wish you a merry Christmas. Quick! Quick!" he said, turning to the ship, and the four-and-twenty white mice scurried down to the cabin and dived into the hold.

Then up on deck they came, staggering under their burdens,

dragging small bales of provisions, little oaken casks, baskets, sacks and hampers. They brought their packages ashore and laid them on the smooth sand near Tom's feet.

There were almonds and raisins, bursting from silken sacks. There were sugar-plums and goodies, pouring out of wicker baskets. There was a host of tiny toys, drums and marbles, tops and balls, pearly shells, and a flying kite, a singing bird and a musical-box.

When the last toy had been safely carried from the ship the white mice scampered back. They weighed anchor, singing "Yo-heave-ho!" and they ran up the rigging. The captain cried "Quack! Quack!" and he stood on the ship's bridge. Before Tom could say "Thank you," the little golden ship began to sail away, with flags flying, and the blue satin sails tugging at the silken cords. The four-and-twenty white mice waved their sailor hats to Tom, and the captain looked at him through his spy-glass.

Away went the ship, swift as the wind, a glittering speck on the waves. Tom waited till he could see her no more, and then he stooped over his presents. He tasted the almonds and raisins, he sucked the goodies, he beat the drum, and tinkled the musical-box and the iron triangle. He was so busy playing that he did not hear soft footsteps behind him.

Suddenly he was lifted up in a pair of strong arms and pressed against a thick blue coat, and two bright eyes smiled at him.

"Well, Thomas, my son! Here I am! You didn't expect me, now did you? A Happy Christmas, Tom, boy. I crept down soft as a snail, and you never heard a tinkle of me, did you?"

"Oh, Father!" Tom flung his arms round his father's neck and kissed him many times. "Oh, Father. I knew you were coming. Look! They've been, they came just before you, in the ship."

"Who, Tom? Who's been? I caught you fast asleep. Come along home and see what Father Christmas has brought you. He came along o' me, in my ship, you know. He gave me some presents for you."

"He's been here already, just now, in a little gold ship, Father," cried Tom, stammering with excitement. "He's just sailed away. He was a duck, Captain Duck, and there were four-and-twenty white mice with him. He left me all these toys."

Tom struggled to the ground, and pointed to the sand, but where the treasure of the fairy ship had been stored there was only a heap of pretty shells and seaweed and striped pebbles. "They's all gone," he cried, choking back a sob, but his father laughed and carried him off, pick-a-back, up the narrow footpath.

On the table in the kitchen lay such a medley of presents that Tom opened his eyes wider than ever. There were almonds and raisins, and goodies in little coloured sacks, and a musical-box with a picture of a ship on its round lid. There was a drum with scarlet edges, and a book, and a pearly shell from a far island, and a kite of thin paper from China, and a love-bird in a cage. Best of all there was a little model of his father's ship, which his father had carved for Tom. "Why, these are like the toys from the fairy ship," cried Tom. "Those were little ones, like fairy toys, and these are big, real ones."

"Then it must have been a dream-ship," said his mother. "You must tell us all about it."

So little Tom told the tale of the ship with blue satin sails and gold mast, and he told of the four-and-twenty white mice with gold rings round their necks, and the Captain Duck, who said "Quack! Quack!" When Tom had finished, his father said, "I'll sing you a song of that fairy-ship, our Tom. Then you'll never forget what you saw."

THE NIGHTINGALE

This is a story about an Emperor of China, who was of course Chinese. It happened many many years ago and that is why you should listen – before the story is forgotten.

This Emperor had the most magnificent palace in the world. It was made of porcelain and decorated all over with the most beautiful paintings and the finest ornaments. The palace gardens were splendid too. The flowers in the flower beds were hung with little bells which tinkled in the wind as you walked by. Everything had been done to make the garden as lovely as possible.

The gardens stretched so far that not even the gardeners knew where they ended. Beyond the lawns with their wonderful borders of flowers there were deep lakes and a thick forest.

The forest extended right down to an inlet of the sea where a poor fisherman kept his boat. In the tall trees near the sea, a nightingale sang each night, and when the fisherman heard it, he would exclaim, "Lord, how beautifully she sings!"

Many travellers came to China. They admired the Emperor's palace of porcelain and his magnificent garden with its tinkling flowers, and they marvelled at the deep lakes and the forests of lofty trees. But when they heard the nightingale sing, they, like the fisherman, would say, "How very beautiful!" And they would add, "The nightingale is the most beautiful thing of all."

When they returned home, some of them wrote books about their travels. And one of these books was sent as a gift to the Emperor of China by the Emperor of Japan. The Emperor took great pleasure in reading about the splendour of his palace, and he sat in his golden chair and nodded his head with approval as he read and read. But when he came to the part about the nightingale, the Emperor stopped in surprise.

"What nightingale?" he exclaimed. "If it is the most beautiful thing in my empire, why do I not know about it?"

He summoned his Lord Chamberlain, who bowed low before

the Emperor and said with great seriousness:

"Your Imperial Majesty, do not believe everything that is written in books. It is probably make-believe," for he had never heard of the nightingale himself and did not wish to seem stupid before the Emperor.

But the Emperor told him that all the other things written in the book were true, so the part about the nightingale must be true also. "Find the nightingale," he ordered, "for I should like it to sing before me tonight."

The Lord Chamberlain asked everyone in the palace, but no one had heard of the nightingale, until someone found a little kitchen maid. She said that she had sometimes heard the nightingale singing when she took scraps of food from the palace kitchen to her family in the evening.

"I will show you where she sings," she offered. Followed by half the Emperor's court, she went through the garden and into the forest down towards the sea.

As they walked, a cow began to moo, and all the courtiers fell to their knees, crying, "Listen to the nightingale! How very beautiful it is!" But the maid laughed and told them it was only a cow. As they passed a lake, they heard some frogs croaking, and once more they fell down and cried out with admiration, "Listen to the nightingale! How sweetly it sings!" But the kitchen maid laughed again and told them it was only frogs they had heard.

At last, they came to a clearing and the little kitchen maid pointed to the nightingale sitting in a tree.

"How strange," said the Lord Chamberlain, "that the nightingale should look so drab and shabby. It is a very ordinary bird." But he had to agree that the nightingale's song was the loveliest sound he had ever heard.

"Little nightingale, will you sing for the Emperor?" asked the kitchen maid.

The nightingale, thinking the Emperor must be among this grand company, said, "Of course, your Imperial Highness," and began to sing again. When she had finished, the Lord Chamberlain explained that the Emperor was waiting at the palace where a great reception was to be held, and it was there that the Emperor wished to listen to the nightingale. "I sing better

in the open air," said the nightingale, but she agreed to go with them to the palace.

They found the Emperor sitting in the middle of a great hall, with a golden perch beside him where the nightingale was to sing. The courtiers stood around dressed in their finest, most colourful clothes, looking at the little grey bird. As the singing began, the Emperor's eyes filled with tears for he had never heard anything so beautiful in his life.

Tears ran down his cheeks as the nightingale sang one song after another, and the little bird was happy, knowing her songs had reached the Emperor's heart. When the nightingale had finished singing, the Emperor offered his own golden slipper, but the nightingale said, "Thank you, but I have reward enough in seeing the Emperor's tears."

After that night the little bird lived in the Emperor's palace in a golden cage. Twice a day, she was allowed to fly in the garden with twelve silken threads tied to her feet, held by twelve courtiers.

The whole city talked of nothing but the wonderful nightingale, and the ladies of the court even put water in their mouths so that they would make a gurgling sound as they talked, like the nightingale's song.

One day a parcel arrived for the Emperor, labelled NIGHTINGALE. When he unwrapped it, he found a beautiful silver and gold nightingale which glittered and sparkled with sapphires, diamonds and rubies. When it was wound up with a little jewelled key, its silver tail went up and down and it sang one of the nightingale's songs. It was a gift from the Emperor of Japan.

Everyone admired the golden nightingale as it sang, first once, then again. Then the Emperor wanted it to sing a duet with the real nightingale, but the real nightingale sang a different song and they did not sound right together. So the court listened to the golden bird while it sang its song thirty-three times.

"Now let my real nightingale sing on her own," said the Emperor at last. But when they looked around, the nightingale was gone! No one had noticed her slip out of an open window and fly off to the forest. "How ungrateful!" everyone exclaimed, and the Emperor banished the nightingale from his empire.

The jewelled nightingale delighted everyone at court. It sparkled all the time and it sang so prettily. The Emperor arranged for the people of his city to hear it on the next feast day and the crowds were charmed by its song. Only the poor fisherman was not quite sure.

"It certainly sings a lovely song," he said thoughtfully, "but when I compare it with the real nightingale I feel there is something missing."

One evening when the golden bird was singing its best for the Emperor and his court, there was a *Whirr* and a *B-rrr* and a *Click*, and the nightingale fell silent. All the best doctors were sent for, but in the end it was the watchmaker who mended the bird. He warned the Emperor that the clockwork was wearing out and advised him not to make the bird sing more than once a day. So the Emperor kept it close to his bedside and listened to it once each evening.

Five years passed and the Emperor lay dying. He was all

alone, for everyone else was preparing for the announcement of the new Emperor. As he lay cold and pale in his great bed, he felt a weight over his heart and, opening his eyes, he saw the figure of Death bending over him. Death was wearing the Emperor's crown; in one hand he held the Emperor's great golden sword, in the other his beautiful banner. Round him floated strange shadowy faces. They were the Emperor's past good and evil deeds, crowding in on him and calling, "Do you remember . . . ? Do you remember . . . ?" The Emperor shuddered and turned away. Then he saw the clockwork nightingale by his bed.

"I must have music!" he cried, hoping to push away the faces and silence their voices. But there was no one to wind up the nightingale, and it sat silent on its golden perch.

Then suddenly, through the window came an exquisite delicate song. On a tree outside was the real nightingale. She had heard the Emperor's call, and come to sing him songs of comfort and hope. As she sang, the Emperor felt stronger and the shadows started to melt away. Death himself listened and, when the nightingale paused, he said, "Go on, little nightingale, go on!"

"I will only sing again if you will give me the Emperor's golden sword, his banner and his Imperial crown," answered the nightingale, and as she sang Death handed back the treasures. Then the nightingale sang of quiet churchyards where white roses grow, where the grass is wet from the tears of those who mourn.

All at once, Death had a great longing to go to his own garden, and he floated out of the window.

"Thank you, thank you, little nightingale," cried the Emperor. "I drove you from my empire, yet you have come back to sing my sins away and take Death from my heart. How shall I repay you?"

"You repaid me," the little bird said, "the very first time I sang to you and drew tears from your eyes. Those are the jewels from the heart that reward a singer. Sleep now, and I will sing to you once more."

As the nightingale sang, the Emperor slept a long and healing sleep. He awoke to find the sun shining through the windows. He was still alone, for his servants thought that he was dead. Only the nightingale was there, outside the window.

"You must always stay with me now," smiled the Emperor, "I shall break that clockwork bird into a thousand pieces."

"Please don't harm it," murmured the nightingale. "It did what it could. As for me, I cannot live in the palace again, but let me come here when I like. Then I will sing to you of those that are happy, of those that are sad, of everything that you cannot see

162

from your palace. A small bird can fly by the poorest fisherman's cottage and the richest house in the land. My songs will make you the wisest of emperors, but one thing you must promise me."

"Anything," replied the Emperor.

"Talk to no one about the little bird who tells you everything."

And so the nightingale flew away. When the servants came in, expecting to see their emperor dead, he stood before them in his royal robes alive and well. And the Emperor turned to them with a smile, and said, "Good Morning!"

THE BLUE LIGHT

There was once an old soldier who fought in many wars for the king. When the fighting was over, this soldier was told to go home. He was given no reward for his efforts so he was feeling miserable as he trudged along. After a time, he came to a dark forest. He followed a little path into the forest and at last he came to a cottage. It was the home of an old witch.

"I'm weary and hungry," the soldier told her. "Could you give me some food and a bed for the night please?"

"Certainly not," the old woman replied, "be off with you."

"I cannot walk any further. Please help me," begged the poor man.

"Well, I'll take pity on you this once," she said, "but in return, you must dig all my garden for me tomorrow."

"I'll do anything you ask," the soldier said. So she gave him a meal and a bed to sleep in.

The next day he kept his promise and he dug the garden very well. The witch was pleased with his work and said he could stay another night if he would chop some wood for her the next day.

The following morning, he chopped the wood and piled it up neatly. This time the witch said to him: "You can stay here one more night, but tomorrow you must bring me the blue light that burns at the bottom of the well."

When morning came she took him outside. She tied a long rope around him and then she let him down into the well. He found the blue light so he tugged on the rope to tell the witch to pull him up. When he was almost at the top she held out her skinny hand.

"Give me the blue light," she said, "I'll look after it now."

But the soldier was clever. "If I give it to her," he thought, "she'll let me drop to the bottom." So he called out, "No, I'll hand over the light when I am safe and sound out of here."

The witch was furious. She let go of the rope so that the soldier and the blue light crashed to the bottom of the well. The poor man fell into thick mud and could not get out.

"Ah well," he said, pulling his pipe out of his pocket, "I may as well enjoy one last smoke."

So he lit his pipe with the blue light and at once a cloud of smoke rose up. Right in the middle of the smoke there was a little dwarf with a feather in his cap.

"What do you wish me to do, master?" he asked.

The soldier was astonished, but managed to say: "Get me out of this well!"

At once the dwarf lifted the soldier, still holding the blue light, to the top of the well. The soldier was delighted. "Thank you," he said. "Can you put the witch into the well now?"

"Certainly," said the dwarf and he dropped her down at once.

They went back to the witch's house where they found many treasures and the soldier quickly packed as much as he could carry. Then the dwarf said: "If you want me, light your pipe with the blue light and I will come at once." Then he vanished.

He almost ran to the nearest town and he looked for a fine inn.

"Get your best room ready for me," he said to the inn-keeper, "and tell the tailor to bring me some new clothes at once." When

this was done, he lit his pipe with the blue light and the little man appeared in the smoke.

"The king sent me home without a penny," the soldier said. "I want to show him who is the master now. Bring his daughter here then I will make her carry out my orders. She can be my servant for the night."

So the dwarf went to the palace where he found the princess sleeping in her room. He picked her up and carried her to the inn. He took her back early next morning.

As soon as the princess saw her father she said: "I had a strange dream last night: I thought someone carried me to a soldier's house and I turned into a servant."

"That is odd," he said. "I'd like to find out if this really happened, so make a hole in your pocket then fill it up with peas. If you are carried along the streets again, the peas will fall out. Then we can follow the line of peas to this soldier's house!"

She did this but the dwarf had been listening too.

That night the soldier asked him to bring the princess to the inn again. The dwarf obeyed but threw peas over many other streets so they were mixed up with the ones which fell from the princess's pocket.

Next day the princess told her father she had seen the soldier again.

"If you are carried away tonight, take a shoe with you and hide it in this soldier's room," the king said. The dwarf heard this and was very worried. So when the soldier asked him to carry off the princess again he said:

"If anyone finds out about this, you will be punished. I cannot save you a second time."

"Stuff and nonsense! I shall be perfectly safe."

"Then," said the dwarf, "you'd better take my advice and leave this town very early in the morning."

The princess carried out her father's plan and she hid her shoe in the soldier's room. As soon as she saw her father next day she told him what she had done. He ordered his soldiers to go to every house and every inn in the town.

The soldiers searched carefully and at last, one of them found the shoe, but the soldier had already left. He had run away but he had not gone far enough. The soldiers soon caught him and dragged him back to the town and he was thrown into a dark, gloomy prison.

The king ordered that the soldier should be executed the next day. The poor soldier then realized that in his hurry to run away he had left behind the precious blue light.

He was full of despair. Suddenly, he saw an old friend walking past. He called to him through the cell bars and asked him if he would collect the blue light and his pipe from the inn. In return he would pay him handsomely. The man readily agreed and soon returned carrying the light and pipe.

"Thank you, thank you, here is your reward," said the soldier gratefully, as he handed his friend several pieces of gold. He then quickly lit his pipe. The smoke rose up and once more his friend the dwarf was at his side.

"I did not listen to you last time, my little friend," said the soldier. "That was very silly of me. Will you still help me?"

"Never fear, master," was the reply. "Do not be downhearted but be of good cheer. You can leave everything to me. But whatever you do, do not forget to carry the blue light, no matter where you are taken." Then he vanished.

The next day a big crowd of people quickly gathered when they heard that the soldier was going to be hanged. The soldier was brought out by guards and as he was led up to the gallows he said to the king:

"Will you grant me one wish?"

"Two, if you like," the king replied just as politely.

"I'd like to smoke one last pipe!" He quickly lit his pipe with the blue light before the king could answer him.

The dwarf appeared. "What are your orders?" he asked.

"Get rid of the guards and all these people. Then cut up the king – into three pieces, if you please!"

The dwarf chased everybody away then ran up to the king with a sword. "Have mercy," begged the king. "I'll give you anything, please don't kill me!"

"Will you give me the princess and make me the next king?" demanded the soldier. The king agreed to this. So in the end the soldier married the princess and became a rich and happy prince.

WHAT THE OLD MAN DOES IS ALWAYS RIGHT

This is a story about an old farmer and his wife who lived happily in a little cottage in the country. The cottage had a thatched roof with a stork's nest tucked in one corner and many sweet-smelling flowers in the garden. Ducks chased each other across a little pond and a horse stood under a shady tree. Neighbours often borrowed this horse to pull a cart or carry loads to market.

One day the old farmer said to his wife, "We do not need a horse as our farm is so small. Why don't we sell him and with the money we get we can buy something useful?"

"That's a good idea, husband. What shall we get?" They sat down and talked for a long time but they simply could not think what to buy.

"Well," said the wife at last, "there is a fair in the town today. You take the horse there and sell it or exchange it for something useful. Whatever you do will be right so get yourself ready to go." She tied his best handkerchief in a smart double bow for him. Then she brushed his best hat and gave him a loving kiss. And the old man rode off on his horse.

It was hot and dusty on the road for many people were riding or walking to the fair. One man was driving a beautiful cow along.

"Why," thought the farmer, "that cow looks as if she gives plenty of good milk. That would be a good exchange – my horse for that cow. I wonder if I can get her?" so he got down from his horse.

"Good morning, friend," he said to the man with the cow. "I'd like to exchange this fine horse for your cow. Do you agree?"

"Certainly," the other man said and he handed over the cow there and then.

The farmer had found something useful and he could have gone home but he wanted to have a look around the fair so he went along the road with his cow. He whistled and the cow mooed and soon they found themselves next to a man who was leading a sheep. It was a nice fat sheep with a thick curly coat.

"I should like to have that sheep," thought the farmer, "we have plenty of grass in the garden and when it is cold a sheep could live in the cottage as it is not as big as this cow. Yes, it will be better to have a nice woolly sheep than a cow!" He stopped and spoke to the shepherd.

"Would you like to take this fine cow in exchange for your sheep?" he asked. The shepherd was surprised, but he agreed to exchange and the old man went on down the dusty road.

Presently, he noticed a man coming out of a field with a big fat goose under his arm.

"That's a fine goose you have there," said the farmer. "It looks heavy too. What lovely soft feathers it has. It would look nice swimming on our pond with the ducks. My wife has always wanted a goose so I could give her this one as a present! Will you take my sheep and I will have your goose?"

The other man was pleased to get such a good bargain so he exchanged his goose for the sheep.

"Thank you very much," said the farmer, and he went cheerfully along the road with the plump goose under his arm.

Next he came to a toll-bridge where everybody had to pay money to go over it. The toll-collector had tied his hen to a tree for he did not want it to fly off over the crowds. This hen had shiny brown feathers and it winked with both eyes all the time.

The farmer thought to himself: "This is the prettiest hen I've ever seen and the cleverest for she can wink!" He walked over to the toll-collector.

"Will you take my goose and let me have your hen?" he asked.

"That's a good exchange," the man said and he tied the goose to the tree and the farmer carried off the hen inside his jacket.

He was hot, tired and hungry by this time so he stopped at an inn. He was stepping inside when he bumped into the landlord, who was carrying a large sack.

"What have you got in there?" the old man asked.

"Rotten apples," answered the landlord. "A whole sack full! I'm taking them to the pigs."

"What a terrible waste! I wish my dear wife could see them for she loves to eat apples."

"Then what will you give me for them?" asked the landlord.

"Why, this fine hen of course." So he handed over his hen and the landlord gave him the sack of apples. He went into the inn and he put the sack down near the hot stove. Then he went to get something to eat and drink. There were plenty of people standing around – farmers, shepherds and two men who were so rich that gold coins kept falling out of their pockets.

The old farmer was eating some bread when there was a hiss – *sss, sss, sss* – which came from near the stove. The apples had started to roast!

"Whatever can that be?" the two rich men asked.

"Well, it's like this," and the old man told them about all the things he had exchanged until he got to the rotten apples.

"Your wife will be furious when you get home," said one man, "you'll get into trouble for your bad bargains."

"Oh no," said the farmer. "She will kiss me and she'll say 'What the old man does is always right'."

"I don't believe you," the man replied, "but let us make a bet. We'll give you hundreds of gold coins if what you say is right."

"If I'm wrong, I've only got this sack of rotten apples to give you, so if I lose I'll give you my house and land."

They all agreed to the bet and they drove off in the men's carriage to the little farmhouse.

"Good evening, dear wife."

"Welcome back, dear husband."

"I've made an exchange."

"I knew you'd manage everything well." The wife hugged her husband but she did not seem to notice the men or the sack.

"I exchanged the horse for a cow."

"That's lovely, now we can have milk, butter and cheese. What a good exchange."

"Yes, but I changed the cow for a sheep."

"Better and better! We have enough grass to feed a sheep. We can have sheep's milk and cheese, warm wool jackets and stockings. You think of everything, dear husband."

"But I changed the sheep for a goose."

"Then we can have roast goose for Christmas and she will look charming on the pond with the ducks."

"But I changed the goose for a hen."

"A hen? She will lay eggs which will hatch into chickens. I've always wanted to keep hens."

"Yes, but I changed the hen for a sack of rotten apples," the farmer said at the end.

"You deserve a big kiss for that," laughed his wife. "After you left this morning I planned a lovely supper for you. Tasty pancakes with herbs. I had some eggs but I'd run out of herbs so I went across to my neighbour. I know she is mean but I only wanted a small handful and she has plenty! I asked her to lend me some. 'Lend?' says she, 'Nothing grows in this garden, not even a rotten apple. There is nothing I can lend you.' Now *I* can lend *her* ten apples, a sackful if she likes!" And the old woman gave the old man a kiss and a hug.

"We like that," the two rich men spoke together. "Whatever he said he'd brought you remained smiling and happy. That is worth a lot of money." They handed over a sackful of gold coins to the old farmer and his wife. But was it the old man or the old woman who was always right?

THE LITTLE TIN SOLDIER

There were once twenty-one tin soldiers who were brothers for they had all been made from one tin spoon. Their splendid uniforms had blue jackets and bright red trousers and they stood smartly to attention carrying their long guns. The first words they heard in this world were: "Tin soldiers!" A happy little boy shouted this as he unwrapped a box on his birthday. He took the soldiers and stood them on the table in a long row.

Each soldier looked exactly the same except for the one standing at the end. He was the last one to be made and there was not quite enough tin to make two legs for him. Still he was able to stand firmly to attention on one leg.

The little boy had plenty of birthday presents – a pink elephant, a funny little train which chug-chugged noisily on the floor, a clown which tumbled over and over, but the finest of all was a wonderful cardboard castle. You could see all the rooms by looking through the little windows. In front there were some small trees dotted around a lake made out of a little mirror with a gold frame and three swans were swimming in this shining water. It was very pretty to look at but the prettiest by far was a little lady who was standing by the lake. She was made out of paper and her dress had many billowing skirts, all made from shimmering muslin. A wide blue ribbon was draped over her shoulder and in the middle of this there was a sparkling tinsel rose, nearly as big as her face. She was a dancer so both arms were stretched out gracefully. She had lifted one leg so far behind that the tin soldier couldn't see it. Why, she seemed to have one leg too.

"She'd be a good wife for me," he thought. "She's so beautiful, even balancing on one toe. But I'm afraid she's very grand for she lives in that castle. I've only got a box and I have to share that with twenty brothers. I couldn't expect her to do that. I must find a way to make friends with her somehow."

All day he hid behind a snuff-box on the table and watched

172

the little ballet dancer.

Later that evening all the tin soldiers were put back in their box except for the one who was still out of sight behind the snuff-box. The people in the house went to bed and now it was the turn of the toys to play their own games. They danced, they threw balls, they visited each other and made such a noise that even the canary in its cage woke up and started to sing. But the soldier with one leg just watched the dancer who was still standing on one pointed toe.

Suddenly the clock struck midnight. The snuff-box lid flew wide open and a wicked goblin jumped up like a Jack-in-the-Box.

"Hey there, tin soldier," cried the goblin, "who do you think you're staring at!" The soldier kept his eyes on the dancer, and said not a word.

"All right," the goblin exclaimed. "Just you wait until tomorrow!"

The next day the boy put his little soldier on the window-sill. Nobody knows whether it was the goblin or the wind that did it, but the window suddenly opened, and the tin soldier fell out, head over heels. Down he went until he landed upside down with his leg sticking straight up in the air and his gun jammed tight between the paving stones.

The little boy rushed outside to look for him. He almost trod on him once but he didn't see him.

If only the soldier had called, 'Here I am!' the boy would have spotted him. "But soldiers in uniform do not shout," he decided.

Now it began to rain, just a little at first and then more and more heavily. People hurried along underneath their umbrellas but no one noticed the upside-down soldier stuck in the stones with the rain pouring over his face and soaking his smart uniform.

When the rain stopped two little boys came running along, jumping over the puddles.

"Oh look!" said one. "Here is a tin soldier. Let's give him a sail." Quickly they made a boat out of some newspaper and stood the soldier in the middle. They popped the boat in the gutter and off he sailed! The boys ran along as well, cheering him on.

The rain had been very heavy so the water was quite deep and rose up in waves. The paper boat bobbed up and down; it swirled and whirled until the tin soldier felt quite sea-sick. He shivered and shook but he looked straight ahead. He still carried his gun

and stood stiffly to attention. All at once the boat sailed into a drain. It became as dark as his box.

"Oh dear, wherever am I going now?" the soldier wondered. "This must be that goblin's idea. Still, if only the little lady with the blue sash could be with me, I wouldn't care if it was twice as dark."

At that moment a large water rat who lived in the drain popped up.

"Give me your passport," said the rat, "you cannot come through here without a passport."

But the tin soldier clutched his gun very tightly and looked straight in front of him and said not a word. The paper boat sailed on and the rat swam hurriedly after it. He gnashed his sharp teeth and called out: "Stop him, stop that soldier!" to the bits of straw and wood floating along. "He hasn't paid me the money to sail in the drain."

The water was flowing very strongly now and the tin soldier could see the daylight where the drain ended. At the same time he heard a fearful roaring noise. To his horror, at the end of the tunnel, the water poured straight out into a canal. The water was flowing so fast that he could not possibly stop the boat. It was hurled into the canal with the tin soldier standing as stiffly as he could. The boat twisted around three or four times then it filled with water. The paper was soaking wet and it began to fall apart. The soldier was up to his neck in water while the boat sank lower and lower until at last the water closed right over the tin soldier's head.

He thought of the pretty little dancer. He would not be able to marry her now. Then the newspaper fell to pieces and the soldier fell out. At that very moment, a big fish swallowed him up. It was much darker inside the fish than it had been inside the drain. There wasn't much room either so the soldier had to lie down, at attention, still holding his gun. The fish darted about, twisting and turning until the poor soldier was feeling quite sea-sick again! It went on swimming to and fro, then at last it lay quite still. Daylight seemed to flash along the fish like lightning then someone called out in surprise:

"Look! A tin soldier!"

The big fish had been caught, taken to the market and there it was sold. Now it was in a kitchen and the cook had cut it open with a long sharp knife before she cooked it for dinner.

The cook picked up the soldier and washed him then she carried him carefully to the sitting-room. Everybody wanted to see this remarkable little man who had been travelling about inside a fish. He was placed on a table where he could be seen easily. The tin soldier stood to attention and stared ahead. He was in the very same room he had lived in before! There was the same little boy, the same toys, even the same snuff-box, but even more important, there was the same beautiful cardboard castle! "How marvellous!" he thought. "There is my beloved dancer too." She was still balancing on one foot with her arms in the air. He wanted to cry little tin tears but he did not think that soldiers should weep, not with all these people watching!

Suddenly, without saying a word to anyone, the little boy picked up the soldier and threw him as hard as he could, right into the middle of the fire. He had no reason or excuse for doing this. Of course, that bad goblin inside the snuff-box was to blame for this terrible deed.

The tin soldier stood there with flames all round him. The heat was tremendous but he was not sure whether it was the fire that was so hot or the love in his heart for the dancer. Out of the flames he looked at the lovely little lady. She looked at him. He could feel that he was melting but he stood to attention, holding his gun stiff and straight.

Then someone opened the sitting-room door and the wind whistled through. The air blew the little lady into the fire next to the soldier. She flared up for a second and then she disappeared.

The tin soldier melted into a small lump and when the servant came to clear out the fire grate, she found him lying there among the ashes in the shape of a little tin heart. But all that was left of the dancer was a tinsel rose, burned as black as coal.

LIZARD COMES DOWN FROM THE NORTH

"Happy days!" said the little green Lizard, flicking his tiny tail in the air. "I'm going to the forest. Oh, happy days!"

And he pattered along on his stumpy legs.

"It's a long, long journey I'm making," he said. "Over bushland and sand and grassland and scrub."

And he hopped in the air with a squeak of delight, because he felt gay and brave and adventurous.

Then Lizard looked up against the sun, and far above him the black-feathered swan beat his wings in the air, and called: "Why are you coming down from the north, you strange little thing with a scaly back?"

But Lizard heard only the beat of strong wings as Swan flew away. So on he pattered.

Black Swan came to the sandy desert.

"I mustn't fly over the sand," he said and he called to Kangaroo Mouse below, "Mouse-with-a-pocket, take my message. Go to the forest and tell them there that a creature is coming down from the north. He has scales on his back, and a flicking tail and he's walking along on his sturdy legs."

Mouse jumped away towards the forest. Faster and faster and faster she raced, until at last her spindle-thin legs were springing so fast that they could not be seen, and she seemed to be a ball of fur, twirling and whirling and blown by the wind.

Then Kangaroo Mouse reached tussocky grassland and stopped. She sat by a tuft of grass and said:

"It's twice as tall as myself *and* my tail, and it's thick and prickly. I can't go on. These kind of jumps are for *real* kangaroos."

"Did you call me?" asked Kangaroo.

"No," said Mouse. "But I'm glad you're here. Go to the forest and take my message. A creature is coming down from the north. He has big shining scales and a beating tail, and he's walking along on his big strong legs!"

Kangaroo leapt towards the forest, crushing the grass beneath his feet. He came to the scrubland, and there he stopped. He saw spiky thickets, and thorny stems.

"Cassowary!" Kangaroo called. And out of the scrub came the great black bird. "Cassowary, take my message. A creature is coming down from the north. He has great shining scales, and a huge beating tail, and he's marching along on his mighty legs."

Cassowary turned to the scrub. He was not afraid of its spikes and thorns.

"I'm a fighting, biting, battling bird. I can push through worse than this," he said.

He pushed and kicked through the spiky scrub, until he saw the forest ahead. He ran through the trees, and before very long he saw Bower Bird, Possum, Platypus, Turkey, and Wombat.

"Listen," he said. "Here is my message. A creature is coming down from the north. He has huge shining scales, and a great lashing tail, and he's crashing along on enormous legs."

The creatures stared at each other, and trembled.

"It's a dragon," said Bower Bird.

"He'll eat us," said Possum.

"Help!" said Platypus.

"Save us," said Turkey.

"What a hullaballoo," said Wombat.

Cassowary stamped his foot.

"You make me angry, you foolish creatures. Talking will do no good," he said. "Why don't you stir yourselves up, and *do* something?"

And he stamped away angrily back to the scrub.

"We must frighten the dragon away," said Bower Bird.

"We must make a scarecrow to scare him," said Possum.

"We don't want to scare a *crow*," said Platypus.

"Then we'll make a scaredragon," Turkey said.

"What a to-do and a fuss," said Wombat.

They stuck the branch of a tree in the ground, for the scaredragon's body. Then they stuck a pineapple on to the branch, for the scaredragon's head.

But still they felt frightened.

"We must hide behind a wall," said Bower Bird.

"And look out over the top," said Possum.

"And when we hear the dragon coming, we'll shout, and wave our paws," said Platypus.

"And make our faces look fierce," said Turkey.

"What a hurry and a scurry," said Wombat.

The creatures began to make a wall.

They stuck a row of sticks in the ground, and Bower Bird, who knew about such things, fixed creepers and stems and twigs between them.

Possum banged the wall with his paw, to see if it was strong and safe.

Platypus filled the cracks with mud.

Turkey scraped up a pile of leaves, building them up behind the wall.

Wombat ran around in circles.

"Now we *ought* to be safe," they said.

They stood in a row on the pile of leaves, looking out over the top of the wall.

And they waited, and waited, and waited.

Into the forest came little green Lizard, flicking his tiny tail in the air.

"Happy days!" he smiled to himself. "I've come to the forest.

Oh, happy days!" And he pattered along on his stumpy legs.

"It's a long, long journey I've made," he said. "Over bushland and sand and grassland and scrub."

He hopped in the air with a squeak of delight, because he felt happy and safe and friendly.

Then Lizard looked up.

He saw the scaredragon.

"What is that pineapple doing?" he said. "Just sitting quite still, all alone, on a stick?"

He saw the wall, and over the top of it, the faces of Bower Bird, Possum, Platypus, Turkey, and Wombat.

"And what are *you* doing, up there?" he asked.

The five faces stared back at little green Lizard.

"We're hiding away from the dragon," said Bower Bird.

"He's coming down from the north," said Possum.

"He'll eat us all up if he can," said Platypus.

"He has huge shining scales and a great lashing tail, and he's crashing along to the forest," said Turkey.

"*What* a time we've had!" said Wombat.

Lizard's small scales shone green in the sun as he flicked his tiny tail in the air. Then he pattered behind the wall, and said:

"Please may I hide behind your wall? I'm not very fond of dragons myself."

So Bower Bird, Possum, Platypus, Turkey, Wombat and Lizard looked out over the top of the wall, waiting for the dragon to come.

And they waited, and waited, and waited.

Far away, a dead branch fell, crashing down to the forest floor.

"The dragon! It's coming," the creatures cried.

They shouted, and flapped their paws about, and made fierce faces, until they were tired.

Then they all said: "Sh!" and "Listen!" and "Hush!"

They kept very still behind the wall, and the only sound they heard was a plop! as a ripe red berry fell to the ground.

"Hurrah!" cried Bower Bird. "We've done it! We've done it! We've scared the dreadful dragon away."

"He's crashing back to the north," said Possum.

"He'll never come *here* again," said Platypus.

"We're really rather clever," said Turkey.

"Clever and brave and fierce!" said Wombat.

Lizard did not say a word. He had disappeared behind a tree.

He looked at his little shining scales, and his flicking tail, and his stumpy legs.

He looked and he thought very hard.

And he guessed.

"Oh my, I'm a dragon, I am!" he said. "Oh ho! I'm a dragon. A great fierce dragon!"

Then Lizard flicked his tiny tail, and he rolled on the ground with his legs in the air, laughing and laughing and laughing.

KING GRISLY-BEARD

There was once a king who had a beautiful daughter. Sad to say she was very proud and haughty. Not one of the princes who wanted to marry her was good enough, she said. Even worse, she was unkind and made cruel jokes about them.

At last the king gave a great feast and he invited anyone who wanted to marry his daughter. Kings and princes came from all over the land. They were enjoying the feast when Princess Lisa came in with her ladies. She walked around and she made rude remarks about each guest, just loud enough for each one to hear.

The first was too fat: "Just like a barrel," she said. The next was too tall: "What a lamp-post," she said. Another one was too short: "Dumpling, dumpling!" she sang. The fourth was too pale. "Pasty-face," he was called. The fifth was over-red: "Turkey-cock," she sneered. She said something nasty to every guest. But she laughed most of all at a good kind king.

"Just look at this one," said the princess, "his beard looks like a raggedy old mop. Let's call him Grisly-Beard!"

The king was shocked at this rude behaviour. He was so upset that he jumped up and in front of everybody he shouted: "You do not deserve a good husband after all these unkind jokes, so listen carefully. Whether you agree or not, you will marry the next beggar who comes to my palace."

The feast ended and a few days later, a poor wandering musician came to the palace and he started to sing.

"Bring that fellow here," the king ordered when he heard him. A rough dirty-looking fellow was brought in and he sang one or two songs in front of the king and Princess Lisa.

"If my songs have pleased you, your Majesty, I beg you to give me a little reward," the musician said.

"You have sung so well that I will give you a big reward – you may have my daughter as your wife!"

The proud princess wept and wailed and begged her father to

182

change his mind. But he would not listen.

"I promised in front of the nobles you insulted that I'd give you to the first beggar who called. I will keep my word."

The beggar and the princess were married at once. It was not a happy wedding and as soon as it was over the king said:

"Now you must get ready to leave. You cannot stay here for you must travel with your husband now."

The beggar led his wife away and before long they came to a great leafy forest.

"Whose is this forest?" she asked.

"It belongs to King Grisly-Beard," answered the beggar, "if you had married him, it would have been yours."

"Poor me," the princess sighed, "I do wish I had married King Grisly-Beard."

They walked on and reached some lovely meadows.

"Whose are these green and flowery fields?" asked the princess.

"They belong to King Grisly-Beard," came the reply, "if you had married him, they would have been yours."

"Poor miserable me," she said. "I do wish now that I had married him."

They travelled on until they came to a fine city.

"Whose is this wonderful city?" the princess asked, though

she knew what the answer would be!

"It belongs to King Grisly-Beard, and if you had married him it would all have been yours."

"Unlucky wretch that I am," she groaned. "Why didn't I choose King Grisly-Beard?"

"Why do you keep wishing for a different husband?" the travelling musician asked. "Am I not good enough for you, my fine lady?" Princess Lisa turned her head away for she could not answer.

Much later, they came to a small cottage.

"What a miserable little house!" the princess said. "Surely nobody could possibly live there! Whoever can it belong to?"

The musician laughed: "That is my house and now it is yours for this is where we are going to live."

"Where are the servants?" she asked.

"Who needs servants?" he replied. "From now on, you must manage things for yourself. Now, be a good wife. Light the fire, boil some water and cook my supper. I'm hungry and tired."

Poor Princess Lisa did not know how to start lighting fires and as for cooking, that was even worse! However, her husband helped her and after some time they were able to have a small supper. The princess did not get much of it so she was still hungry when she went to bed.

Next morning her husband woke her very early.

"The house needs a good clean and there is no one to do it – except you," he said cheerfully.

She didn't feel at all cheerful as she swept and dusted – very badly it must be said.

After a few days which seemed like years to her, they had eaten all the food in the cottage and they had only a few coins left.

"Wife," said the beggar, "this won't do. We cannot go on spending money when we are not earning any more. I get money by singing songs to rich people. Now it is your turn. There are plenty of willows outside and I can teach you to weave them into baskets."

He went out and cut the willows and brought them home. He showed her what to do but it made her fingers very sore.

"I can see that making baskets doesn't suit you," he said.

"Perhaps you'd better try spinning."

He handed her some cotton and she tried hard to spin it. She didn't know how to do it properly so the threads cut her fingers until they started to bleed.

"Oh dear," her husband said crossly, "you can't weave, you can't spin, you can't clean, you can't cook. You can't do anything! But I have another idea to get some money. You can go to the market-place and sell some pots and pans for me."

So off she went. At first, things went well for people liked buying from such a beautiful girl. Then suddenly, a drunken man appeared and rode his horse against her stall. Every single pot was shattered. She wept bitterly.

"What will happen?" she wondered as she ran home. "Whatever will my husband say to me!"

"How could you be so silly! Fancy getting in the way of a horse," he exclaimed. "Dry your eyes for I've found you more work. You are to be a kitchen maid at the king's palace."

So the princess went off to do the dirtiest work in the palace kitchens.

Not long afterwards there was a grand wedding-feast at the palace. The princess stayed in the kitchen. She was a much humbler person now and was sorry for her unkind ways. Suddenly, a handsome man in golden robes came into the kitchen. He seized her hand.

"You must be my partner in the dance," he said.

"Sir, I cannot. I am a kitchen-maid." She was terrified. It was King Grisly-Beard and she dared not disobey a king!

"Don't be afraid," he said gently. "Don't you know me? I am the beggar-musician from the cottage and I am the one who broke all your pots at the market-place to teach you a lesson. I did these things because I love you. I know you are truly sorry for what you did. Dear wife, let us forget what has happened before for this is *our* wedding feast!"

Ladies brought silken robes for her and to her joy, her father arrived with all his courtiers. They were delighted with the change in the princess and enjoyed the wedding feast. And King Grisly-Beard and Lisa, his queen, lived in great happiness thereafter.

DICK WHITTINGTON AND HIS CAT

There was once a poor boy called Dick Whittington who lived in a small village in the south of England. He had no proper home for both his parents had died, and he was unkindly treated by many of the villagers. One day, Dick overheard someone say that the streets of London were paved with gold, and he decided that he would go there at once and pick his fortune up in gold pieces from the streets, for he thought people might treat him more kindly if he were rich.

So young Dick set out to walk to London. He had not gone far when a man in a cart stopped and asked him if he was running away from home. "I have no home," Dick answered. "I am on my way to London to find my fortune."

"I'm going to London myself," said the carter. "Jump up here beside me and we will journey together."

They arrived in London just before nightfall, and the carter left Dick and made his way to an inn. Poor Dick stood alone and looked around him in dismay. Where was all that fine gold? All he could see were dirty streets and lots of unfriendly people. He had nowhere to sleep and in the end he spent the night in the corner of an alley where he hoped he would come to no harm.

The next morning Dick woke up cold, miserable and very hungry. He wandered around begging for food, but again and

again people shouted at him, "Go away you lazy rascal! Be off with you," and aimed angry blows at his head. At last he collapsed in the street, and lay there, too weak to look further for food.

By chance, Dick had fallen in front of a house belonging to a rich merchant called Mr Fitzwarren. The cook was trying to drive Dick away, when Mr Fitzwarren returned home from inspecting his ships. He stopped and said to Dick, "Why don't you work if you need food?"

"I would work," said Dick, "but I know nobody who will give me anything to do."

"Take him into the kitchen," Mr Fitzwarren ordered the cook. "Feed him first and then find some work for him."

So Dick was given a home and a living. He had a small corner of the attic to sleep in and his job was to help the cook with all the pots and pans in the kitchen. Dick's life should have been much better than before, but he still had two difficulties to face.

The first was that the attic he slept in was overrun by rats and mice. At night they scampered all over him and kept him awake. After a time he solved this problem by saving the few pennies he was paid, and buying himself a cat. In no time at all, the cat chased away all the rats and mice and Dick was able to sleep peacefully.

The other difficulty, which was not so easy to overcome, was the cook's bad temper. She shouted and screamed all day, and would scold Dick and hit him with a wooden spoon, even when he was working as hard as he could.

One night Dick decided he could stand it no more. Early the next morning before the cook was up, he set out with his cat to seek his fortune elsewhere. The two of them walked as far as Holloway, on their way out of London, then Dick sat down on a stone to rest. It was the first of November, All Saints' Day, and the church bells were ringing. As Dick sat and listened it seemed they were ringing out a message for him:

> *Turn again Whittington,*
> *Thou worthy citizen,*
> *Lord Mayor of London.*

"Lord Mayor of London?" said Dick. "I should like to be Lord Mayor and ride in a fine coach. I can put up with a few scoldings from the cook if that is what is in store for me." So Dick and his cat retraced their steps to Mr Fitzwarren's house. Luckily they were able to slip back before they had been missed.

Now Mr Fitzwarren used to send ships far across the sea to trade with other countries. He would load a ship with goods for the captain and ship's crew to sell in faraway places and then they would bring back goods that could be sold at home.

One day he called his household together. "I am sending a ship to the African coast to trade," he said. "Would any of you like to send something of yours on it? You can then share in the profits if the voyage is successful." Everyone produced something except for Dick, who had nothing to offer. "Have you nothing of your own, Dick?" asked Mr Fitzwarren kindly, and Dick replied, "Only my cat."

"Then let your cat go on the ship," said Mr Fitzwarren. His daughter, Alice, said, "Dick loves his cat. Let me put something in for him." But her father said, "No, it must be his, not something belonging to someone else."

So Dick fetched his cat and said goodbye to it sadly. The captain of the ship was delighted, for the cat was an excellent mouser, and so he had no trouble with rats and mice on his voyage.

After some months the ship arrived at a place on the African coast called Barbary, where people called the Moors lived. The

captain sent a message to the king to say he had fine goods for sale, and he was invited to the palace to show them. While he was talking to the king and queen some dishes of food were brought in, but almost immediately rats and mice ran up and, before the captain's eyes, ate all the food. The captain was astonished, and asked if this was what normally happened.

"Alas, yes!" came the reply. "The country is suffering from a plague of rats and mice, and we cannot get rid of them."

"I think I may have the answer on my ship," said the captain, and he sent a message asking for Dick's cat to be brought to the palace. More food was laid out, and the rats and mice appeared as before. The cat immediately pounced, killing at least a dozen before they scattered. Everyone was delighted, and the queen asked, "What do you call this animal?"

"Puss is the name she answers to," said the captain, and when the queen called, "Puss, puss," the cat went over to her and purred. The queen was a little alarmed at first, as she had seen how fiercely the cat had attacked the rats and mice, but the captain told her not to be anxious. "Puss is very friendly with people," he said, "and would soon rid your kingdom of rats and mice."

"I would give great wealth to own this animal," said the queen.

So the captain began bargaining, and it was agreed that the king would buy the whole cargo from Mr Fitzwarren's ship and pay a fine price for it, and for the cat alone the king paid ten times the sum again.

When the ship came back to the Port of London, the captain showed Mr Fitzwarren the gold and jewels he had brought from Barbary and told him the story of the cat. The merchant sent for Dick. "From now on, Dick," he said, "we should all call you Mr Whittington, for you are a rich man." Mr Fitzwarren then paid him all the money the captain had received for the cat.

From this time on Dick worked with Mr Fitzwarren, and became a successful merchant himself. He married Mr Fitzwarren's daughter Alice, and three times he was elected Lord Mayor of London. He was also in time knighted by the king and became Sir Richard Whittington. He was not only famous, but he was popular too for he always helped the poor with his money. Sometimes when he was old he would tell his grandchildren the story of his cat, and how the bells of London had called him back when he was only a poor boy:

Turn again Whittington,
Thou worthy citizen,
Lord Mayor of London.

EE-AW! EE-AW!

Once upon a time there lived a very happy family. The man was lazy, his wife was lazy, but the son was the laziest of all. He never did anything all day long.

His father and his mother loved their son. Whatever he wanted to do made them feel happy. They only worried if he was not well, but this did not happen very often.

He grew into a tall, strong and handsome young man who was always cheerful and everybody liked him. However, his parents began to wonder what would happen to their son. As the father was lazy, he did not earn much money so he could not get enough food for the three of them. They did not want their son to find any work for he liked doing nothing.

"Beggars don't work, dear wife," said the husband. "People give them all they need. Shall our son become a beggar?"

"What an excellent idea. That would suit our dear boy very well," his wife replied.

The young man was happy to try anything, so off he went, stick in hand and a bag on his back. It was a lovely day so he did not hurry as he wasn't going anywhere in particular.

It wasn't very long before he began to feel hungry, so he sat down and ate the food his mother had packed for him. His walk had made him rather sleepy so he lay down in the shade and took what he said was going to be a little nap. But it was getting dark when he awoke so he thought he had better start walking and think about begging for a night's shelter. He still didn't hurry and as he walked along the road he met an old woman.

"Good evening," she said. "Where are you going?"

"I'm going begging," he said. "Work doesn't agree with me, you see. And now I must beg someone to give me a room for the night."

"Well, you are truthful at least," said the old woman. "I'll show you the way to a good resting place. Go into the first house

you see on your left hand side. Do exactly as I tell you and you'll be allowed to stay there. Now listen carefully: just outside the door you will see a little stone, pick it up and put it in your pocket. When you are asked to go inside, you must answer 'Many thanks' to everything you hear, no matter what it is. Then when the others in the house are asleep, you must put the little stone on the hearth, underneath the warm ashes.''

"Thank you," said the young man. He yawned as he strolled along. He felt like having another rest! He noticed the house on his left-hand side and he picked up the little stone next to the front door.

He knocked on the door and a woman came out.

"Good evening," he said. "I beg you, can you give me a night's lodging?"

"Oh no, I can't do that," said the woman.

"Many thanks," he replied.

"I've just told you that I can't," said the woman, "we don't admit strangers at night."

"Many thanks," and the young man walked inside and sat down on a bench.

The woman could not push him out. He was not doing any

harm so she let him sit there. Soon her husband came home.

"Who is that?" he whispered to his wife.

"I have no idea," the wife replied. "He must be very stupid for I told him he couldn't stay and all he said was 'Many thanks'."

The man went over to the table and his wife brought in a big bowl of soup. It smelt delicious. "Eat as much as you can," she said, "and I'll keep the rest for later." She didn't even look at the young man, but he jumped up.

"Many thanks, many thanks," he said and he sat down at the table as well. He helped himself from the bowl and he left very little for the poor husband and wife. They were surprised but said nothing.

"Go to bed if you're tired," the wife said to her husband a little later. "Many thanks," said the beggar and he took off his clothes and jumped into the warm bed.

The man and his wife were speechless but before they could do anything the beggar was snoring. They were too kindhearted to turn him out so they slept on the floor.

As soon as they were asleep the young man opened his eyes. He crept quietly to the hearth and he hid the little stone in the ashes. Then he went back to bed and slept soundly.

The people who owned the house had a very cheerful daughter. She always got up early in the morning and her first job was to light the fire. On this morning she picked up the poker and stirred the ashes. Then she put on plenty of sticks but she could not make them catch fire. She bent down and opened her mouth to blow, but all she could say was: "Ee-aw! Ee-aw! Ee-aw!" It was a horrible noise. And she could not stop making it. The fire would not burn and all she could do was sit down and cry: "Ee-aw! Ee-aw! Ee-aw!" This funny noise woke up her mother.

"Whatever is the matter?" she called.

"It's . . . ee-aw!" the girl sobbed. "The fire – ee-aw, ee-aw, ee-aw!"

"Well if the fire won't burn, there's no need to make that noise." The mother grumbled as she got dressed. Then she came into the room and went to the hearth.

"This fire needs a good blow," she said. She poked the ashes, put on some more sticks and as she bent down to blow, "Ee-aw! Ee-aw! Ee-aw!" she cried. It really was a horrible noise. She could not stop making it either and the fire still did not burn.

Mother and daughter were now shouting together and the noise woke up the husband.

"Have you gone mad in there?"

"Ee-aw! Ee-aw! Ee-aw!" was their loud reply.

So he got dressed and went over to the hearth.

"What a fuss both of you are making. Can't you manage to light a fire!" He picked up the poker, he stirred up the ashes and as he bent down to blow: "Ee-aw! Ee-aw! Ee-aw!" He sounded just the same as his wife and daughter. All three stood and screamed together.

They waved their arms and somehow they made a plan.

"Ee-aw . . . daughter . . . go . . . ee-aw," it sounded like. But somehow they decided that she should run to the doctor and ask him to come and help. The girl ran as fast as she could to the doctor's house and she tried to give her message clearly.

"Please – ee-aw! My father says 'Ee-aw!' and mother says 'Ee-aw!' Will you please come – ee-aw – to our house – ee-aw – and see if you can help us. Ee-aw, ee-aw, ee-aw!"

The doctor was puzzled. He thought the girl must be unwell so he went back with her. He listened to the father and mother and he guessed that a witch must have put a spell on the fire. He picked up the poker and poked among the ashes. At once the same thing happened. He could say nothing but 'Ee-aw' over and over again.

The girl was sent to the village again, and this time she went to find the priest. She was out of breath when she arrived at the church and this is what she said:

"A witch – ee-aw – has got into our house – ee-aw! Will you come at once – ee-aw – with your book – ee-aw – and say some magic words – ee-aw – that will break the spell. Ee-aw! Ee-aw!"

The priest picked up his book, put on his long robe and followed the girl to her home.

The doctor, the father and the mother were all standing around the hearth. The fire was not burning, and they were still shouting 'Ee-aw' at the top of their voices. The priest looked at the fire then opened his mouth but all that came out was:

"Ee-aw! Ee-aw! Ee-aw!"

Everybody was upset. What could they do now? The father managed to say that his daughter would marry any man who could cure them.

"I'll give him – ee-aw – all my goods when I die – ee-aw – as well," he promised.

All this time the young man had stayed calmly in bed. He listened to all the noise but he was too lazy to move. He heard the promises of the father.

"I can marry this lovely girl and get a good house to live in," he thought.

So he jumped out of bed and ran to the hearth. He snatched the little stone out of the ashes, dashed to the door and threw it far away across the fields. Then he turned to the girl, took her hand and kissed her.

At once the spell was broken. The sticks caught fire and the fire blazed brightly. There was a lot of noise as everybody started talking and laughing at the same time. The father and the mother hugged their daughter and they were so happy that they kissed the young man as well!

The young man never went out begging again, for soon after this he and the girl were married and they lived long and happily together.

HOW THE WHALE BECAME

Now God had a little back-garden. In this garden he grew carrots, onions, beans and whatever else he needed for his dinner. It was a fine little garden. The plants were in neat rows, and a tidy fence kept out the animals. God was pleased with it.

One day as he was weeding the carrots he saw a strange thing between the rows. It was no more than an inch long, and it was black. It was like a black shiny bean. At one end it had a little root going into the ground.

"That's very odd," said God. "I've never seen one of these before. I wonder what it will grow into."

So he left it growing.

Next day, as he was gardening, he remembered the little shiny black thing. He went to see how it was getting on. He was surprised. During the night it had doubled its length. It was now two inches long, like a shiny black egg.

Every day God went to look at it, and every day it was bigger. Every morning, in fact, it was just twice as long as it had been the morning before.

When it was six feet long, God said:

"It's getting too big. I must pull it up and cook it."

But he left it a day.

Next day it was twelve feet long and far too big to go into any of God's pans.

God stood scratching his head and looking at it. Already it had crushed most of his carrots out of sight. If it went on growing at this rate it would soon be pushing his house over.

Suddenly, as he looked at it, it opened an eye and looked at him.

God was amazed.

The eye was quite small and round. It was near the thickest end, and farthest from the root. He walked round to the other side, and there was another eye, also looking at him.

"Well!" said God. "And how do you do?"

The round eye blinked, and the smooth glossy skin under it wrinkled slightly, as if the thing was smiling. But there was no mouth, so God wasn't sure.

Next morning God rose early and went out into his garden.

Sure enough, during the night his new black plant with eyes had doubled its length again. It had pushed down part of his fence, so that its head was sticking out into the road, one eye looking up it, and one down. Its side was pressed against the kitchen wall.

God walked round to its front and looked it in the eye.

"You are too big," he said sternly. "Please stop growing before you push my house down."

To his surprise, the plant opened a mouth. A long slit of a mouth, which ran back on either side under the eyes.

"I can't," said the mouth.

God didn't know what to say. At last he said:

"Well then, can you tell me what sort of a thing you are? Do you know?"

"I," said the thing, "am Whale-Wort. You have heard of Egg-plant, and Buck-Wheat, and Dog-Daisy. Well, I am Whale-Wort."

There was nothing God could do about that.

By next morning, Whale-Wort stretched right across the road, and his side had pushed the kitchen wall into the kitchen. He was now longer and fatter than a bus.

When God saw this, he called the creatures together.

"Here's a strange thing," he said. "Look at it. What are we going to do with it?"

The creatures walked round Whale-Wort, looking at him. His skin was so shiny they could see their faces in it.

"Leave it," suggested Ostrich. "And wait till it dies down."

"But it might go on growing," said God. "Until it covers the whole earth. We shall have to live on its back. Think of that."

"I suggest," said Mouse, "that we throw it into the sea."

God thought.

"No," he said at last. "That's too severe. Let's just leave it for a few days."

198

After three more days, God's house was completely flat, and Whale-Wort was as long as a street.

"Now," said Mouse, "it is too late to throw it into the sea. Whale-Wort is too big to move."

But God fastened long thick ropes round him and called up all the creatures to help haul on the ends.

"Hey!" cried Whale-Wort. "Leave me alone."

"You are going into the sea," cried Mouse. "And it serves you right. Taking up all this space."

"But I'm happy!" cried Whale-Wort again. "I'm happy just lying here. Leave me and let me sleep. I was made just to lie and sleep."

"Into the sea!" cried Mouse.

"No!" cried Whale-Wort.

"Into the sea!" cried all the creatures. And they hauled on the ropes. With a great groan, Whale-Wort's root came out of the ground. He began to thrash and twist, beating down houses and trees with his long root, as the creatures dragged him willy-nilly through the countryside.

At last they got him to the top of a high cliff. With a great shout they rolled him over the edge and into the sea.

"Help! Help!" cried Whale-Wort. "I shall drown! Please let me come back on land where I can sleep."

"Not until you're smaller!" shouted God. "Then you can come back."

"But how am I to get smaller?" wept Whale-Wort, as he rolled to and fro in the sea. "Please show me how to get smaller so that I can live on land."

God bent down from the high cliff and poked Whale-Wort on the top of his head with his finger.

"Ow!" cried Whale-Wort. "What was that for? You've made a hole. The water will come in."

"No it won't," said God. "But some of you will come out. Now just you start blowing some of yourself out through that hole."

Whale-Wort blew, and a high jet of spray shot up out of the hole that God had made.

"Now go on blowing," said God.

Whale-Wort blew and blew. Soon he was quite a bit smaller. As he shrank, his skin, that had been so tight and glossy, became covered with tiny wrinkles. At last God said to him:

"When you're as small as a cucumber, just give a shout. Then you can come back into my garden. But until then, you shall stay in the sea."

And God walked away with all his creatures, leaving Whale-Wort rolling and blowing in the sea.

Soon Whale-Wort was down to the size of a bus. But blowing was hard work, and by this time he felt like a sleep. He took a deep breath and sank down to the bottom of the sea for a sleep. Above all, he loved to sleep.

When he awoke he gave a roar of dismay. While he was asleep he had grown back to the length of a street and the fatness of a ship with two funnels.

He rose to the surface as fast as he could and began to blow. Soon he was back down to the size of a lorry. But soon, too, he felt like another sleep. He took a deep breath and sank to the bottom.

When he awoke he was back to the length of a street.

This went on for years. It is still going on.

As fast as Whale-Wort shrinks with blowing, he grows with sleeping. Sometimes when he is feeling very strong, he gets himself down to the size of a motor-car. But always before he gets himself down to the size of a cucumber, he remembers how nice it is to sleep. When he wakes, he has grown again.

He longs to come back on land and sleep in the sun, with his root in the earth. But instead of that, he must roll and blow, out on the wild sea. And until he is allowed to come back on land, the creatures call him just Whale.

THE FAIRY WIFE

Many years ago a young man called Demetros lived with his mother in the land of Greece. His job was to look after a herd of goats. Behind their small house there was a little stream and every day Demetros's mother filled a big jar with water which she carried back on her shoulder. She called it the Fairy Spring but no one knew why.

One day she was ill so Demetros went for the water after he had put his goats into their shed. The moon was shining and he saw three girls sitting by the stream. He filled his jug and did not look at them for he thought they were just shepherdesses from the village.

Suddenly a cock crowed loudly. At once the girls stood up, joined hands and danced over the hills. They whirled faster and faster until they vanished in a puff of smoke.

Demetros was puzzled. Who were they? They could not be girls from the village. Where had they disappeared to? He went home but he did not tell his mother what he had seen. He thought about the girls the next day while he watched his goats and he hurried to fetch water again that night. This time six maidens were sitting there but as soon as the cock crowed they rose to their feet and danced away.

Demetros filled his jug and walked home.

"You are quiet tonight," his mother said. "Have the goats run away with your tongue?"

"It's nothing, mother," he replied. Then a little later, he could not keep quiet.

"Twice I have been for water," he said, "and twice I've seen strange girls who vanish when the cock crows."

"Be careful, my son," she said. "That stream is a Fairy Spring and those girls are fairies. I am afraid they may harm you."

Demetros went to the stream a third time. This time nine maidens danced away when the cock crowed.

"They cannot harm me if I only look at them, they are so lovely!" thought Demetros as he walked home with his eyes on the hills.

"Where is the water?" his mother cried. "The fairies made you forget it, I see. Tomorrow, my son, there is a full moon when fairies are dangerous so you must keep away from the stream."

Demetros decided to listen to his mother's advice.

"I will not go to collect water tonight. I do not wish to see wicked fairies."

When he put his goats into their shed the moon was shining brightly and he could not help thinking about the beautiful girls once more. He stayed in the shed until midnight then he tried to go home but his legs and feet carried him to the stream instead and he could not stop or turn around. This time ten maidens were waiting and the tenth was the loveliest of all. When they saw Demetros they joined hands and made a circle around him. They sang sweetly and danced so lightly that their feet did not touch the ground.

Demetros longed to dance with them.

"Come and join us," they begged. "Come Demetros, come."

"Come and live in our palace," said the tenth and loveliest fairy, "you will be happy with us."

She held out her hand and Demetros went with them as they danced over the hills. He forgot about his mother and his goats in their shed for he did not want to leave the golden-haired fairy ever again. She danced towards him and he put out his hand to catch her but he only managed to take her silken handkerchief. The dancing stopped instantly and all the fairies screamed. Then like a sudden gust of wind they disappeared. The tenth one sank to the ground and hid her face in her hands. She cried bitterly and Demetros knelt down to dry her tears but she pushed him away.

"Do not touch me. You cannot help me," she sobbed. "My friends have left me because you have taken my handkerchief!"

Poor Demetros. He put away his own handkerchief and walked away. He looked back and saw that she was following him. He stopped and so did she. He walked on and she walked after him. They walked like this, stopping and starting, until they reached his house.

His mother was surprised to see the golden-haired girl standing there but she welcomed her kindly for she guessed that

Demetros loved her. He handed her the fairy handkerchief which she wrapped up carefully and then put away in a special box.

The beautiful fairy was called Katena. Demetros loved her very much and they soon became man and wife. Katena was a good wife. She was kind and gentle and she worked hard. She liked to spin, weave and embroider. All her work was very fine and delicate – far better than anything the villagers could do. After a time she had a beautiful baby girl with golden hair like her own. The baby was called Neraidokoretso – a long name which means 'daughter-of-a-fairy' or 'fairy-child'. Demetros called her Nera for short.

Everybody liked the fairy-wife for she worked hard and well but she was not happy. She did not sing or dance and she rarely spoke. She never laughed, even at Demetros's little jokes. This made him sad, though his mother tried hard to make Katena feel happy.

One day, on a special Greek holiday called St Konstantino's Day, Demetros's mother went to visit her cousin. As soon as she left the house Katena suddenly said:

"It is a holiday today, husband. I should like to go to the village to join your friends. It is a long time since I've danced.

Please bring me my prettiest dress. And could you get my special handkerchief as well? Then we can dance together as we did under the full moon years ago."

Demetros was overjoyed. If his wife wanted to dance she must be feeling happy for she had never spoken like this before. He rushed to the cupboard and pulled out the first dress he saw and then he looked around till he found the beautiful handkerchief in his mother's box.

As soon as Katena was ready, Demetros took his little daughter's hand and the three of them ran down to the village.

The villagers, dressed in their best clothes, were laughing and dancing on the grass. They stood in a circle and faced each other and held the corner of a handkerchief stretched between them. Katena and Demetros joined the circle and they did the same with the fairy handkerchief. First the couples danced together then the girls went one by one into the middle of the ring. When it was Katena's turn, Demetros dropped his side of the handkerchief. At once Katena took it and jumped into the centre, whirling and twirling and singing a strange song. Three times she danced round the villagers then she rose to the sky and floated away. Demetros felt in his heart that his fairy wife had gone and would never come back.

When his mother heard the sad news she said gently: "My son, you must be brave. This is magic work, and there is nothing you can do about it. She is not from this world and would never have been truly happy – her home is with the other fairies."

Demetros tried to be cheerful but he now worried that his little daughter would be unhappy without her mother. Every day she left the house and hurried off to the fields. She talked and sang to herself, and no one understood the words she used.

Nera's grandmother was troubled because the little girl never seemed to be hungry so one day Demetros followed her to see what she did all day. First she went to the Fairy Spring but she did not touch the water. She held up her arms and looked towards the sky. She called and at once a white mist covered her. Demetros heard a voice coming from the mist and when his daughter answered, he could not understand a single word! He went back to the house and told his mother what he had seen.

"I'm sure it was Katena," he said. "When Nera goes off alone, her mother comes from the sky to talk to her. I think she brings fairy food and this is why Nera is never hungry."

Demetros was troubled. One day he turned to his mother and said: "I have the strangest feeling that something dreadful will happen soon."

"What do you mean?" she asked.

"I am afraid that Nera may not stay with us. She will dance away as well."

These words saddened the grandmother for she loved the girl very much.

Then on a lovely summer's day, Nera's fifteenth birthday, she went up to the Fairy Spring and Demetros followed her as he had done many times before. She held up her arms to the sky and a shimmering white cloud covered her. But this time the cloud lifted her up and carried her up and away over the hills. Demetros heard two sweet voices singing softly as the cloud disappeared and he knew that Nera had joined her mother.

Demetros wandered over hills and through woods, wishing he could see his fairy wife and child again. He realized, though, that they were happier in their fairy world and at last returned home to where his mother was waiting for him.

THE SELFISH GIANT

Every afternoon, as they were coming from school, the children used to go and play in the Giant's garden.

It was a large lovely garden, with soft green grass. Here and there over the grass stood beautiful flowers like stars, and there were twelve peach-trees that in the springtime broke out into delicate blossoms of pink and pearl, and in the autumn bore rich fruit. The birds sat on the trees and sang so sweetly that the children used to stop their games in order to listen to them. "How happy we are here!" they cried to each other.

One day the Giant came back. He had been to visit his friend the Cornish ogre, and had stayed with him for seven years. After the seven years were over he had said all that he had to say, for his conversation was limited, and he determined to return to his own castle. When he arrived he saw the children playing happily together in the garden.

"What are you doing here?" he cried in a very gruff voice, and the children ran away.

"My own garden is my own garden," said the Giant; "anyone can understand that, and I will allow nobody to play in it but myself." So he built a high wall all round it, and put up a noticeboard,

TRESPASSERS WILL BE PROSECUTED

He was a very selfish giant.

The poor children had now nowhere to play. They tried to play in the road, but the road was very dusty and full of hard stones, and they did not like it. They used to wander around the high walls when their lessons were over, and talk about the beautiful garden inside. "How happy we were there!" they said to each other.

Then the spring came, and all over the country there were little blossoms and little birds. Only in the garden of the Selfish Giant it was still winter. The birds did not care to sing in it as there were no children, and the trees forgot to blossom. Once a beautiful flower put its head out from the grass, but when it saw the notice-board it was so sorry for the children that it slipped back into the ground again and went off to sleep. The only people who were pleased were the Snow and the Frost.

"Spring has forgotten this garden," they cried, "so we will live here all the year round."

The Snow covered up the
grass with her great white cloak,
and the Forest painted all the trees
silver. Then they invited the North Wind to stay with them, and
he came. He was wrapped in furs, and he roared all day about the
garden, and blew the chimney-pots down. "This is a delightful
spot," he said. "We must ask the Hail on a visit." So the Hail
came.

Every day for three hours he rattled on the roof of the castle till
he broke most of the slates, and then he ran round and round the
garden as fast as he could. He was dressed in grey, and his breath
was like ice.

"I cannot understand why the Spring is so late in coming,"
said the Selfish Giant, as he sat at the window and looked out at
his cold, white garden; "I hope there will be a change in the
weather."

But the Spring never came, nor the Summer. The Autumn
gave golden fruit to every garden, but to the Giant's garden she
gave none. "He is too selfish," she said. So it was always Winter
there, and the North Wind and the Hail, and the Frost, and the
Snow danced about through the trees.

One morning the Giant was lying awake in bed when he
heard some lovely music. It sounded so sweet to his ears that he
thought it must be the King's musicians passing by. It was really
only a little linnet singing outside his window, but it was so long
since he had heard a bird sing in his garden that it seemed to him
to be the most beautiful music in the world. Then the Hail stopped
dancing over his head, and the North Wind stopped roaring, and
a delicious perfume came to him through the open casement. "I
believe the Spring has come at last," said the Giant; and he

jumped out of bed and looked out.

What did he see?

He saw a most wonderful sight. Through a little hole in the wall the children had crept in, and they were sitting in the branches of the trees. In every tree that he could see there was a little child. And the trees were so glad to have the children back again that they had covered themselves with blossom, and were waving their arms gently above the children's heads. The birds were flying about and twittering with delight, and the flowers were looking up through the green grass and laughing.

It was a lovely scene, only in one corner it was still winter. It was the farthest corner of the garden, and in it was standing a little boy. He was so small that he could not reach up to the branches of the tree, and he was wandering all round it, crying bitterly. The poor tree was still covered with frost and snow, and the North Wind was blowing and roaring above it. "Climb up, little boy," said the Tree, and it bent its branches down as low as it could; but the boy was too tiny.

And the Giant's heart melted as he looked out. "How selfish I have been!" he said; "Now I know why the Spring would not come here. I will put that poor little boy on the top of the tree, and then I will knock down the wall, and my garden shall be the children's playground for ever and ever." He was really very sorry for what he had done.

So he crept downstairs and opened the front door quite softly, and went out into the garden. But when the children saw him they were so frightened that they all ran away, and the garden became winter again. Only the little boy did not run, for his eyes were so full of tears that he did not see the Giant coming. And the Giant stole up behind him and took him gently in his hand, and put him up into the tree. And the tree broke at once into blossom, and the birds came and sang on it, and the little boy stretched out his two arms and flung them around the Giant's neck, and kissed him. And the other children when they saw that the Giant was not wicked any longer, came running back, and with them came the Spring. "It is your garden now, little children," said the Giant, and he took a great axe and knocked down the wall. And when the people were going to market at twelve o'clock they found the giant

playing with the children in the most beautiful garden they had ever seen.

All day long they played, and in the evening the children came to the Giant to bid him good-bye.

"But where is your little companion?" he said; "The boy I put into the tree." The Giant loved him best because he had kissed him.

"We don't know," answered the children: "he has gone away."

"You must tell him to be sure and come tomorrow," said the Giant. But the children said that they did not know where he lived, and had never seen him before; and the Giant felt very sad.

Every afternoon, when school was over, the children played with the Giant. But the little boy whom the Giant loved was never seen again. The Giant was very kind to all the children, yet he longed for his first little friend, and often spoke of him. "How I would like to see him!" he used to say.

Years went over, and the Giant grew very old and feeble. He could not play about any more, so he sat in a huge armchair, and watched the children at their games, and admired his garden. "I have many beautiful flowers," he said; "but the children are the most beautiful flowers of all."

One winter morning he looked out of his window as he was dressing. He did not hate the Winter now, for he knew it was merely the Spring asleep, and that the flowers were resting.

Suddenly he rubbed his eyes in wonder and looked and looked. It certainly was a marvellous sight. In the farthest corner of the garden was a tree quite covered with lovely white blossoms. Its branches were golden, and silver fruit hung down from them,

and underneath it stood the little boy he had loved.

Downstairs ran the Giant in great joy, and out into the garden. He hastened across the grass, and came near to the child. And when he came quite close his face grew red with anger, and he said, "Who hath dared to wound thee?" For on the palm of the child's hands were the prints of two nails, and the prints of two nails were on the little feet.

"Who hath dared to wound thee?" cried the Giant; "tell me that I may take my big sword and slay him."

"Nay," answered the child: "but these are the wounds of Love."

"Who art thou?" said the Giant, and a strange awe fell on him and he knelt before the little child.

And the child smiled on the Giant, and said to him, "You let me play once in your garden, today you shall come with me to my garden, which is Paradise."

And when the children ran in that afternoon, they found the Giant lying dead under the tree, all covered with white blossoms.

THE SNOW-MAIDEN

There was once a poor man called Ivan who lived with his wife, Marousha, in a very cold country. They were a happy couple but they would have loved to have had a child and so they would often watch the children from the houses nearby.

One winter's day the snow was deep and sparkling all around the village. Ivan and Marousha watched the families throwing snowballs and sliding in the snow. They were enjoying themselves very much and the children laughed happily. Then they began to make a snowman and Ivan and Marousha watched as they made it bigger and bigger.

"Wife," said Ivan suddenly, "why don't we go outside and make a snowman too?"

"That's a splendid idea," she replied. "We can enjoy the fun as well! But husband, why must we build a big *snowman*? We haven't got a child of our own so let us make a snow-child."

So they went out into their little front garden. First they rolled some snow along and made a little body. Then they made little arms, hands, legs and feet. When these were finished they rolled and smoothed a snowball until it looked like a head. They put a nose and a chin on the snowy head, and found two pretty stones to use for eyes. They had just finished and were standing back to take a good look at the snow-girl when Ivan gave a shout.

"Look, she moved! The snow-girl moved!" and at that moment he felt a warm breath touch his cold cheeks. He looked closer. The snow-maiden's eyes were now the brightest blue he had ever seen. Her lips were pink, her cheeks were rosy and she was smiling a beautiful smile! She shook her head and when the snow fell off, the couple could see that she had golden curly hair. She moved her arms and then her legs just like a real little girl.

"Ivan! Ivan!" Marousha cried. "Heaven has smiled on us this day for this is our very own child." She bent down and hugged and kissed her as though she would never let her go.

"Your name will be Snegourka for that means 'snow-maiden'," she went on. In the meantime Ivan picked up the little girl and carried her inside their house. Marousha sang and laughed because she was happy and both husband and wife watched Snegourka every hour of the day.

She grew taller and prettier all the time. Many children came to visit the snow-maiden and they showed her their toys and taught her how to play many games. They chattered and sang songs and the little house was always filled with visitors and happy noises.

Snegourka was very clever and learned quickly how to do many things in the house. She spoke softly and sweetly and everybody liked her. She played in the snow just like the other children and she liked to make houses, animals and sledges from snow and ice.

At last the long bitter winter ended. The sun came out and started to warm the frozen gardens. The snow melted and sweet-smelling spring flowers and green grass grew once more. The village children were happy because they could take off their heavy coats and boots. They danced and sang but the snow-maiden sat by the window; she looked sad and would not join in the games outside.

"What is the matter, little daughter?" asked Marousha. "You do not look happy. Perhaps you are not feeling well today?"

"Please do not worry about me," she replied in her sweetest voice. "I'm quite well and there is nothing wrong with me but I do not want to go outside."

The snow-maiden would sometimes play hide and seek with her friends but she did not like leaving her dark hiding places to come out into the warm sun. She would often sit under the shady trees on the river bank. Best of all, she enjoyed thunder and lightning and she clapped her hands and laughed when hail stones fell around her.

One lovely summer's day the children in the village decided to go for a walk in the woods and Snegourka went with them. It was very warm in the sunshine and the children ran along the path to the woods.

"Let us see how fast we can run," said one little boy. "Come along everybody, follow me!"

They ran and ran when all of a sudden they heard a tiny sigh coming from behind them. They looked around. There was nobody there. They looked again. They could not see the snow-maiden. She was not following them.

"Snegourka, where are you?" they called. No one answered. "Snow-maiden, do not hide from us. Tell us where you are." They looked everywhere but they could not spot her. In the end, the children sadly went home.

Next day all the villagers looked for the snow-maiden. Along every path they went and they looked under every bush but they found nothing at all. Ivan and Marousha cried out loudly: "Snow-maiden, snow-maiden, come back to us!" Sometimes they thought they could hear a faint sweet voice from the shady places.

When the snow and ice return to that land, perhaps the snow-maiden will return to Ivan and Marousha. Who knows!

KING MIDAS

Midas, the richest king in the world, was sitting on his throne one day when he wished that he had so much gold it could not be counted. Just then, a shepherd came in.

"Your Majesty," he said, "I found this old man wandering in the fields. He is cold and hungry."

"Why, it is Silenus, the friend of Bacchus, the God of the Fields," the king said. "You are welcome to rest in my palace, old man." So Silenus stayed with King Midas and was treated very well. After a few days, Midas took the old man home. Bacchus was overjoyed to see him for he felt sure that Silenus had died in the fields. He turned to Midas and said:

"Ask for whatever you like and I will give it to you." Midas could not believe his ears. At last he could have as much gold as he wanted!

"I'd like everything I touch to turn into gold," he said. "Everything!"

"Very well," Bacchus said, looking surprised, "but will that make you happy?"

"Of course it will," said the greedy king.

"Then you may have your wish," Bacchus said.

Midas went back to his palace and on the way he longed to see if his wish had come true. He pulled a branch off a tree. It turned into pure gold! Midas was delighted so he touched his clothes. They turned into gold but they were so heavy that he could hardly walk. He picked up some stones and they were pure gold so he ordered his servants to collect every single one of them.

Midas reached the palace gardens and he picked a sweet-smelling red rose. It turned yellow and hard in his hand so he changed every bush into ugly yellow lumps.

"How beautiful they look now!" he exclaimed. "And all this gold belongs to me."

He went into the palace. "I am hot and dusty," he said.

"Bring me water that I may wash. Then prepare the table for I am hungry too."

Servants carried in a bowl of cool water but when Midas dipped his fingers in, the water changed into golden ice. He sat down to eat and the cloth, plates, glasses all turned to gold. He picked up some bread. It turned into gold. He snatched some meat. The same thing happened. He seized an apple but before he took a single bite, it became hard and heavy.

Midas wanted a drink but as soon as the wine touched his lips it turned into liquid gold. He gazed at all the wonderful food for he could not eat the smallest crumb. He was so hungry that he grabbed a tiny fish but it turned into glittering gold in his hand.

He went outside, trying to forget about food. He was miserable and this made him bad-tempered so when he saw a gardener standing on the path Midas pushed him out of the way. The man turned into a gold statue which could not move or speak. Midas was horrified. He did not know what to do and at that moment his beautiful daughter came running up to him. He loved her dearly so he hugged and kissed her. Instantly she changed into a little gold statue.

"Speak to me," he begged, "run and jump, do anything you like." But the little gold figure did not say a word!

Midas was the richest and the unhappiest man in the world. He could not eat or drink and his daughter could not move. He decided to visit Bacchus but he could not move quickly as he was wearing solid gold clothes.

"Why have you come to see me?" Bacchus asked when he saw Midas. "Did you not get your wish?"

"Oh yes," said Midas, "but I want you to take back your promise! I am hungry and thirsty. My lovely daughter is a statue in the garden. I am the unhappiest king alive!"

"I asked if gold would make you happy," Bacchus said. "Gold was what you wanted so do not complain to me."

"I know now it was wrong of me to love gold so much." Midas fell on his knees. "I am truly sorry that I was so greedy. Please, please take back your gift."

Bacchus sighed. "I see that you are filled with sorrow. Go therefore to the River Pactolus and touch the water there." Midas called 'thank you' over his shoulder for he was already running to the river. He dived into the cool water which turned yellow all around him. He touched some grass as he climbed out. It stayed soft and green. He picked up stones and they did not change in his hand.

Midas thought of his daughter so he borrowed a jug from a shepherd and filled it with water from the river. He took it to the palace and threw some over his daughter and then over his poor gardener. They came alive at once!

Filled with joy, Midas went inside and sat down. "Take these gold dishes away," he ordered, "and bring me the plainest ones you can find. And bring bread and water to me." The servants were surprised but they obeyed the king's orders. "This is the finest food I have ever tasted," laughed Midas. The king was never greedy again for he knew that all the gold in the world had not given him happiness.

THE UGLY WIFE

In England many years ago King Arthur ruled over the Knights of the Round Table.

One day a lady came to King Arthur's court. Her clothes were torn and her eyes were wild. "My husband has been taken away by a wicked knight," she cried. "I ask you, King Arthur, to kill him and then bring my husband back."

The king decided to find this evil knight himself so he set off on his horse at once. Presently a black castle came into view and a knight in black armour rode towards him.

"Who are you?" King Arthur demanded.

"I am Gromer, servant of your enemy, Queen Morgan le Fay," was the answer. "She came to your court and pretended that I, the Black Knight, had carried off her husband. You came to rescue him but I am going to kill you instead."

"But that is not fair. If you are a true knight, you should kill me in a fair fight," King Arthur said angrily.

"I will not fight you but I will give you a chance," he said. "In return you must promise to come here in a year with the answer to this question: 'What do women want most in the world?' If you cannot give me the proper answer you will die a fearful death." He laughed horribly as he clanked away.

The king returned to his court and asked Gawain, one of his best knights, to help him. They asked many women the same question but they got many different answers. Gold, jewellery, a good husband, even strawberry jam!

There was only one day left when they came across an old woman near a river. She was wearing a wonderful gown covered with sparkling jewels. She lifted her head. What a shock! She was the ugliest woman he had ever seen. Her teeth were yellow and broken; her lips drooped down to her chin. Her nose was squashed flat and her eyes rolled wildly round but worst of all, she was fat. She was like a barrel with hands and feet stuck on.

King Arthur bowed politely because she was a woman but before he could speak she made an odd crackling noise.

"I know your question already," she screeched, "and I know the answer. I'll tell it to you on one condition."

"What may that be?" the king asked.

She looked at Gawain. "Your knight is young and handsome. I think I'd like him as my husband. I'll save your life if he will marry me."

Gawain was shocked. What would his family say if he married this monster? Then he remembered that Gromer was hoping to kill the king the next day. "Your Majesty," he groaned, "if it will save your life . . ."

"It certainly will," the ugly woman cackled.

"Then of course I must marry her."

"I cannot let you do this," the king cried.

"You cannot stop me," Gawain said. He turned to the woman, "If you can save the king, I promise, on my honour as a knight, that I will marry you. Now tell him what women want most of all."

Next day Arthur rode to the castle. He shivered as the Black Knight came out with his sword already uplifted.

"What is the answer to my question? Answer correctly or you die!" The king said clearly: "Women want their own way in all things." The Black Knight dropped his sword, his armour fell off and he knelt before the king. "That is the true answer! You have broken the spell which the wicked queen put on me. She made me wear black armour. She wanted me to kill you. Forgive me, your Majesty, and allow me to be one of your knights."

The king was astonished but he agreed. So they rode back to the court together.

On seeing the king's safe return, Sir Gawain kept his promise to the ugly woman and they were married at once. At the wedding feast the ugly bride gobbled her food and spilt wine over her beautiful dress. She was rude to the wedding guests and fell over their feet. The king and the knights were very polite and tried to pretend that they had not noticed anything!

When the feast was ended, Gawain and the fat old woman were alone in their room. "Why are you so miserable on your

wedding day?" she demanded. He did not want to reply, but she demanded an answer.

"Lady," he said at last, "I do not wish to upset you but here is the truth: you are old, ugly and ill-mannered. I cannot love you. I only married you to save the king."

"I am old but that may make me wiser," she said in her crackly voice, "and people sometimes are ugly outside but inside they have a kind heart. Gawain, you are a noble knight. Will you teach me how to behave please?"

He did not know what to say at first. "Lady, you are right," he said gently. "You saved the king from death so I will try to help you if I can."

As he was speaking, the ugly woman melted away and a most beautiful girl now stood in front of him.

"You have broken the spell!" she exclaimed. "The Black Knight who was set free by King Arthur, is my brother. Your kind words have saved me from the wicked magic of Morgan le Fay. Will you choose me for your wife now?" and she smiled sweetly.

The astonished Gawain took her hand. "With all my heart."

The king held another wedding feast the next day. Everybody said it was a wonderful day and Gawain and his lady lived happily together for many more years.

THE LITTLE MATCH GIRL

Many years ago on the day before Christmas, all the streets in the city were covered with snow.

An icy cold wind was blowing as a little girl tried hard to push her way through the snow. It was getting dark and she was a long way from home. She was wearing a shabby dress with many holes in it and there was a thin black shawl around her shoulders which did not keep out the wind at all. That morning she had borrowed her mother's shoes which were much too big for her. When she hurried across the road to get out of the way of a horse and cart, the shoes slipped off. They were soon hidden under the snow and the little girl never saw them again.

Her feet turned blue with cold as she walked slowly along. She clutched a match box in one hand and some matches wrapped in an old rag in the other. She had not sold even one single match all day. By this time lighted lamps were appearing in house windows and there was a lovely warm cooking smell of roast goose in the air. People with baskets of food and presents hurried past the little girl. They smiled and called 'Happy Christmas' to their friends as they went into their cosy houses.

The little girl's head and shoulders were covered with snow flakes and at last she could not walk any further. She felt ill because she was so hungry and sank into a corner between two big houses. She tucked her frozen toes under her ragged dress and rubbed them as hard as she could. The poor girl was too scared to go home without selling any matches and now her hands seemed to be frozen like her toes. She decided to light one little match to try and warm her fingers so she struck one on the house wall. There was a sudden light and the girl held her fingers near the flame. It made her think of a big stove with a bright warm glow. She stretched out her toes to warm them. Then the flame went out. The warm stove vanished and all that was left was a burnt out match.

Snow was still falling and she felt too tired to shake it off. She struck another match and at once the wall next to her turned into glass. By the tiny flame, she could see right inside the room. There was a table which was covered with good things to eat. She sniffed the air. It was full of savoury smells and suddenly she saw a roast turkey flying towards her. It was brown and juicy and there were roast potatoes all around it. There was even a knife and fork and plate. She put out her hands to take them. Then the match went out. Everything disappeared. The poor little girl was still sitting by the cold grey wall, and she could not stop shivering. She curled up in a ball to try and get a little warmer. But it was no use, so she lit a third match. Its tiny flame showed the room inside the same house. But now she thought she was inside the house herself. There was a beautiful Christmas tree with lots of presents lying underneath it. The tree was covered with silver balls, bright glowing candles and tiny jingling bells. Her hand went up to touch them. At that moment the match went out. The Christmas candles lit up the room then they shot up into the night sky and turned into twinkling stars. As she watched, she saw the brightest star of all fall back to the earth.

"Someone, somewhere is dying," the little girl whispered when she saw the star fall from the sky. "My dearest grandmother told me all about this just before she died. She said that a soul goes to heaven whenever a star falls from the sky."

Quickly she lit another match. And as it burned with a tiny bright flame, her grandmother appeared by her side. She was smiling sweetly and her eyes looked at her little half-frozen grand-daughter with love and pity.

"Oh dearest grandmother," the little girl sobbed, "please don't disappear like the warm stove, the roast turkey and beautiful Christmas tree! Don't go, I beg you. Take me with you. Please take me too."

With shaking fingers she lit every single match in her ragged bundle. She wanted so much to keep her grandmother near her. The matches burned so brightly this time that the dark night turned into day. The grandmother held out her arms and very gently she lifted the little girl and held her closely. Then ever so slowly and carefully they flew up into the sky. They flew higher and higher until they reached a place where there was no trouble or worry but only peace and happiness.

The next morning in the passage between the houses someone found the little girl almost covered with sparkling snowflakes. Her feet were tucked up underneath her skirt and her shawl was pulled tightly round her shoulders. But on her frozen lips there was a sweet smile. In her hand she clutched an empty match-box.

"Oh how sad," all the people said "to be outside all night in this freezing weather! She must have tried to warm herself with her matches. Poor little girl."

They did not know that the little girl was smiling because she had seen such beautiful things as her spirit floated calmly away on that Christmas Eve so long ago.

THE STORY OF PERSEPHONE

This story is one of the tales that the ancient Greeks told about their gods. It is the story of Persephone, the lovely daughter of Demeter, Goddess of the Harvest.

Demeter travelled round the world with Persephone, talking to the trees and plants that produce food. As she passed the plants and touched them, they grew and flourished, and their fruit ripened. On hot days as she walked through a field of corn, the husks would swell and the corn would turn golden as she passed by. Whenever she visited orchards and vineyards, the apples, peaches, pears and grapes would be sweet and ready to eat. Persephone, who loved to go with her mother, would dance with joy to see how lovely the flowers looked when Demeter passed by.

One day Persephone asked her mother if she could go and play with her friends on the mountainside, while her mother went about her work. Demeter agreed, but warned Persephone not to stray too far. Then she went to visit some valleys where the harvest was late. Persephone and her friends scrambled happily over the mountainside. They found many flowers growing in the mountain meadows, and began to pick them, making garlands and chains as they wandered. Further and further they went, calling out to each other when they found a gentian, a lily or a mountain rose, until they were a long way from the valley where they had started.

Soon the meadows were shimmering in the hot mid-day sun. Persephone dropped behind her friends and sat on the grass to rest and to finish the garland she was making.

Suddenly there was a roar and a rushing sound. The side of the mountain seemed to split open and out galloped six great black horses, pulling a gleaming black chariot. Persephone was terrified and called out, "Mother, mother, help me!" But even as she called, the man driving the chariot leant out and swept Persephone up into the chariot. He pulled at the reins to turn the

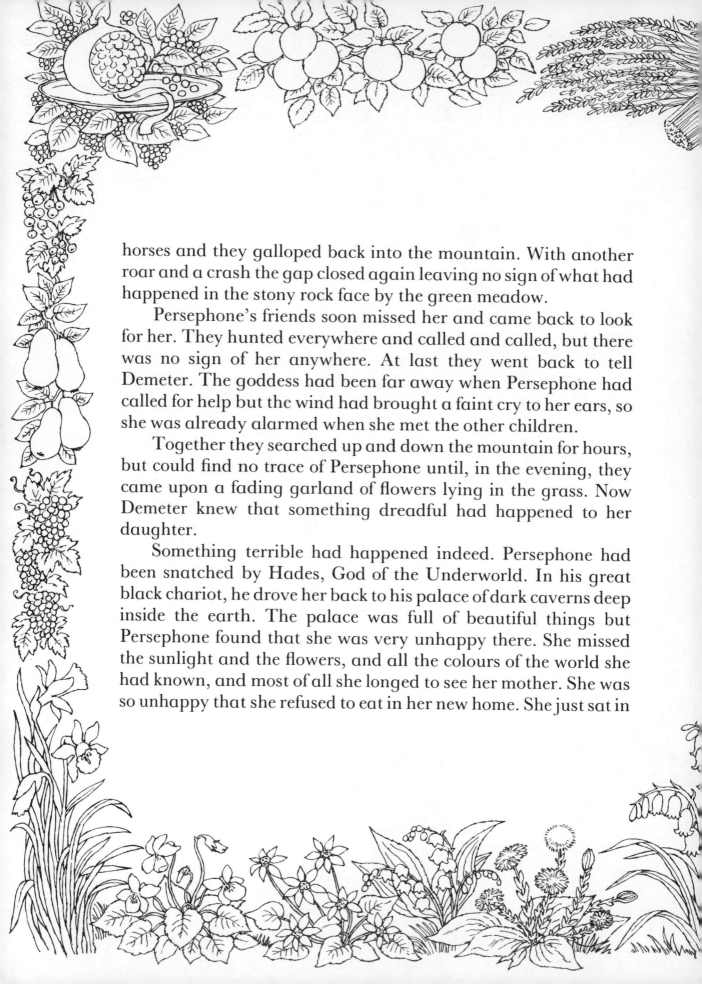

horses and they galloped back into the mountain. With another roar and a crash the gap closed again leaving no sign of what had happened in the stony rock face by the green meadow.

Persephone's friends soon missed her and came back to look for her. They hunted everywhere and called and called, but there was no sign of her anywhere. At last they went back to tell Demeter. The goddess had been far away when Persephone had called for help but the wind had brought a faint cry to her ears, so she was already alarmed when she met the other children.

Together they searched up and down the mountain for hours, but could find no trace of Persephone until, in the evening, they came upon a fading garland of flowers lying in the grass. Now Demeter knew that something dreadful had happened to her daughter.

Something terrible had happened indeed. Persephone had been snatched by Hades, God of the Underworld. In his great black chariot, he drove her back to his palace of dark caverns deep inside the earth. The palace was full of beautiful things but Persephone found that she was very unhappy there. She missed the sunlight and the flowers, and all the colours of the world she had known, and most of all she longed to see her mother. She was so unhappy that she refused to eat in her new home. She just sat in

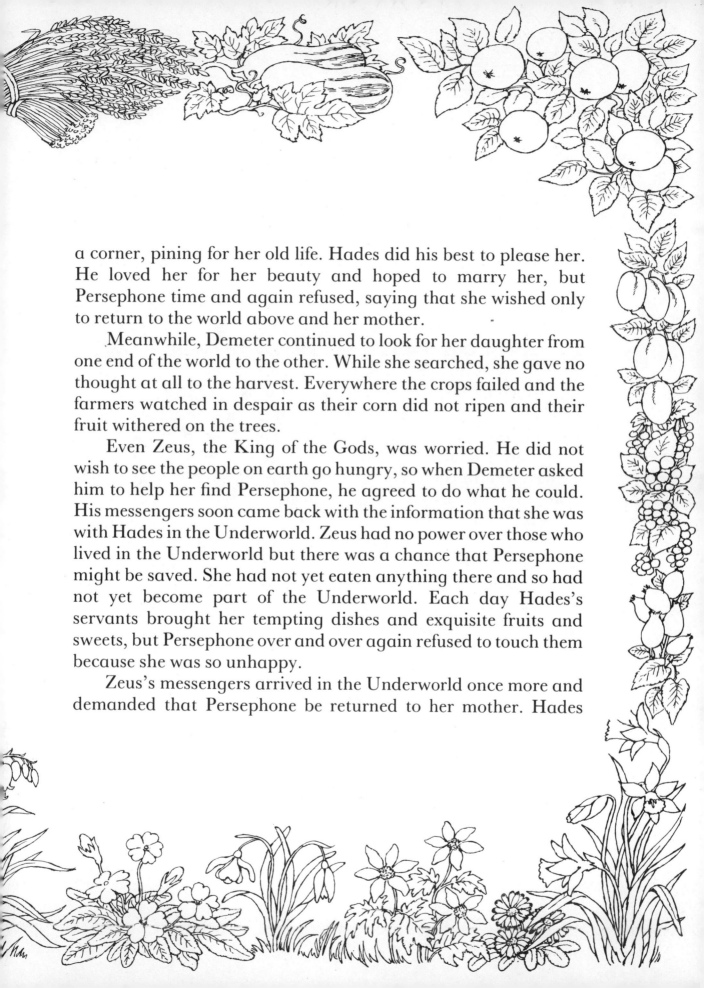

a corner, pining for her old life. Hades did his best to please her. He loved her for her beauty and hoped to marry her, but Persephone time and again refused, saying that she wished only to return to the world above and her mother.

Meanwhile, Demeter continued to look for her daughter from one end of the world to the other. While she searched, she gave no thought at all to the harvest. Everywhere the crops failed and the farmers watched in despair as their corn did not ripen and their fruit withered on the trees.

Even Zeus, the King of the Gods, was worried. He did not wish to see the people on earth go hungry, so when Demeter asked him to help her find Persephone, he agreed to do what he could. His messengers soon came back with the information that she was with Hades in the Underworld. Zeus had no power over those who lived in the Underworld but there was a chance that Persephone might be saved. She had not yet eaten anything there and so had not yet become part of the Underworld. Each day Hades's servants brought her tempting dishes and exquisite fruits and sweets, but Persephone over and over again refused to touch them because she was so unhappy.

Zeus's messengers arrived in the Underworld once more and demanded that Persephone be returned to her mother. Hades knew that unless he could make her eat he would lose the lovely girl he wanted to marry. He ordered his servants to prepare a bowl of beautiful fruit and he himself carried it to Persephone. On the top he put a sweet-smelling pomegranate which he knew was her favourite fruit. Persephone, after much coaxing, reluctantly ate six seeds from the pomegranate for she felt Hades had been kind to her and did not want to hurt his feelings. Then she turned her head away and refused to eat anymore, for the taste reminded her of the sunshine and the happy carefree life that she missed so much. But Hades was triumphant, knowing that, because she had taken food, she belonged forever to the Underworld.

Demeter was heartbroken. She grieved so much at the loss of her daughter that she had no heart to travel the earth as goddess of the harvest, and people began to grow hungry. Zeus was sorry for Demeter and for the people of the earth, so he sent his messengers to Hades once more. Because he knew Persephone was unhappy, Hades decided that she should spend six months of each year, one for each pomegranate seed she had eaten, in the Underworld, but that for the remaining six months, she should return to the earth and join her mother.

And so it has been ever since. You will know when Persephone is in the Underworld with Hades as leaves fall and plants wither and die. These months we call Autumn and Winter. When Persephone returns to the earth her mother, Demeter, is overjoyed and in her happiness makes the flowers open and new shoots spring from the ground. Crops flourish and fruit ripens to produce food. These six months when Persephone once more dances through the fields and orchards with her mother we call Spring and Summer.

RUMPELSTILTKSKIN

One day a king was riding through a village in his kingdom when he heard a woman singing,

"My daughter has burnt five cakes today,
My daughter has burnt five cakes today."

It was the miller's wife who was cross with her daughter for being so careless. The king stopped as he wanted to hear her song again. The miller's wife hoped to impress the king so she sang,

"My daughter has spun fine gold today,
My daughter has spun fine gold today."

And she boasted that her daughter could spin straw into gold thread.

The king was greatly impressed.

"If your daughter will spin for me in my palace, I'll give her many presents. I might even make her my queen," he announced.

"What a wonderful chance," muttered the miller's wife under her breath. "We'll all be rich." Then out loud she said, "My daughter will be honoured, your Majesty."

The king took the girl back to the palace. He ordered a spinning wheel to be placed in a room filled with straw.

"Spin this into gold by the morning or you will die," he commanded. Left alone, the poor girl wept bitterly. She could not spin straw into gold as her mother had boasted and she could not escape as the king had locked the door firmly behind him.

Suddenly a little man appeared from nowhere. He had a small pointed face and wore elfin clothes in green and brown.

"What will you give me, pretty girl, if I spin this straw into gold for you?" he asked.

"I will give you my necklace," the girl replied, "if you really can help me. Yet how can anyone do this task!"

At once the little man sat down by the spinning wheel. Singing strange songs, he spun all the straw into fine gold thread. Then taking the girl's necklace, with a skip and a hop and a stamp of his foot, he disappeared.

When the king unlocked the room the next morning he was astonished and delighted to see the skeins of golden thread. He sent delicious food to the miller's girl. But that evening he took her to another room with an even bigger pile of straw and a spinning wheel.

"Now spin this into gold," he ordered, "and I shall reward you well. But if you fail I shall chop off your head." He walked out, locking the miller's daughter in behind him.

The poor girl stared at the straw and the spinning wheel. "What can I do now?" she cried, "I cannot turn straw into gold and the king will kill me if I fail."

Suddenly the same little man in elfin clothes stood before her.

"What will you give me this time if I spin your gold for you?"

"I'll give you my bracelet," said the miller's girl for she had nothing else to offer.

At once the little man set the spinning wheel whirring. Singing his weird songs, he quickly turned the straw into golden thread. Before dawn he had finished, and snatching the bracelet he was gone, with a skip and a hop and a stamp of his foot.

The king was delighted the next morning, and sent pretty clothes and good food up to the girl as a reward. "If this girl can really spin gold from straw," he thought greedily, "I shall always

be rich if I make her my wife. But in case there is some trick I will try her once more."

So the third night the king took the miller's girl into another room with an even greater pile of straw and a spinning wheel.

"Spin this into gold," he commanded. "If you succeed, I shall marry you and you shall be queen. If you fail your head will be chopped off tomorrow."

Once more, as the girl wept bitterly before the pile of straw and the spinning wheel, the little man appeared from nowhere.

"I see you need my help again," he said. "How will you reward me this time if I save your life?"

"I have nothing to give," the miller's daughter said sadly. "Perhaps you should just go and leave me to my fate."

"Ah!" said the little man, "But if the straw is spun into gold tonight, you will become the queen. Will you promise to give me your first child when it is born?"

"Yes! Yes!" cried the girl. When this time came, she was sure she could save her child somehow.

So the little man sat and twirled the spinning wheel, beating

his foot on the floor and singing his strange songs. Then with a skip and a hop and a stamp of his foot, once more he was gone.

The next day the king was delighted to see the gold spun from the huge pile of straw and he kept his promise. The miller's daughter became his wife and queen.

And as queen the miller's daughter forgot all about her promise to the little man. About a year later, a fine son was born, and she was horrified when one day the little man appeared.

"I have come to claim the child you promised me," he said, stamping his foot as he spoke.

The queen pleaded with him to release her from the promise.

"Take my jewels and all this gold," she begged, "only leave me my little son."

The little man saw her tears and said, "Very well. You have three days in which to guess my name. You may have three guesses each night. If you fail on the third night, the baby is mine." Then he vanished.

The queen sent for all her servants and asked them to go throughout the kingdom asking if anyone had heard of the little man and if they knew his name. The first night the little man came she tried some unusual names:

"Is it Caspar?" she asked.

"No!" he said and stamped his foot in delight.

"Is it Balschazzar?"

"No!" he said as he stamped his foot again.

"Is it Melchior?"

"No!" he cried. He stamped his foot and disappeared.

The next evening the queen thought she would try some everyday names. So when he appeared she asked,

"Is your name John?"

"No!" he said with his usual stamp.

"Is it Michael?"

"Is it James?"

"No! No!" he cried, stamping his foot each time. Then with a hop and a skip, triumphantly he disappeared.

The next day the queen was very sad for she could not see how she could guess the little man's name. She felt sure she would lose her baby that night.

The palace servants came back without any news except for one who returned to the palace towards the end of the day. He went straight to the queen and told her that at the very edge of the kingdom, under the mountains, he had seen a little man singing as he danced around a fire.

"What did he sing?" asked the queen breathlessly.

"Today I brew, tomorrow I bake,
Next day the queen's child I take.
How glad I am that nobody knows
My name is Rumpelstiltskin."

The queen clapped her hands with joy and rewarded the servant. That night the little man appeared and asked if she had guessed his name.

"Is it Ichabod?"

"No!" he cried with pleasure as he stamped his foot.

"Is it Carl?"

"No!" he shouted as he laughed and stamped his foot.

"Is it . . ." the queen hesitated . . . "Is it Rumpelstiltskin?"

Now it was the queen's turn to laugh. The little man stamped his foot so hard it went through the floor. He disappeared in a flash and was never seen again.

THE FISHERMAN AND THE BRASS BOTTLE

There was once a poor fisherman who never had enough money to buy food for his wife and three children. Every day he went fishing but he never cast his nets into the sea more than four times. He believed it would bring him bad luck if he did it more often.

One day he took his nets down to the shore and threw them out for the first time. When he started to pull them in they felt heavy. "That is good," he thought, "there must be a lot of fish here." But when he pulled the nets on to the beach all he could see was a dead donkey.

He cast his nets into the sea a second time and once again they were very heavy. He tugged and heaved them out of the water but this time all he found was a large broken jar which tore the nets. He was disappointed but mended his nets and tried again a third time. Alas, the nets filled up with stones and seaweed and shells.

The poor fellow stood by the water's edge. "This is my last chance," he said. "I can only throw my nets once more today," and he threw them as far as he could into the waves. He waited a short time then he drew them in. It was hard work and the fisherman felt sure his luck had changed. He looked quickly but there was not a single fish there. Instead he saw a big bottle made of brass. It was tightly fastened with a thick seal made of lead. The fisherman took it out of the net and looked at it closely.

"I am sure I can sell this bottle in the market for the seal has a picture of the great King Solomon on it," he said to himself. He shook the bottle but nothing rattled inside. "There must be something there," he thought, "I'd better open it and take a look."

He took out his knife and cut open the seal. Then he turned the bottle upside down and gave it another shake. Nothing happened. Then suddenly thick smoke poured out and the man

watched in amazement as it covered the beach and the sea then spread out until it covered the sky. When all the smoke had left the bottle it turned into a Genie, twice as big as the biggest giant in the world. It was very ugly and the terrified fisherman tried to run away but his legs would not move. Then the Genie came alive!

"Solomon, Solomon, do not kill me!" the Genie cried. "Please forgive me and from now on I will do whatever you command!"

"Whatever are you saying?" said the fisherman. "Don't you know that King Solomon has been dead for more than a thousand years?"

"Don't speak to me like that," the Genie said fiercely, "or I will kill you."

"Why do you say that?" said the poor fisherman. He was frightened for the Genie was bigger than anything he'd ever seen. "I rescued you from the bottom of the sea and I let you out of that bottle. You should be thanking me not shouting at me!"

"In what way shall I kill you?" was the cruel reply.

"First, tell me why you want to kill me."

"I must kill you because of a promise I made," the Genie answered. "Listen carefully, then you will understand. King Solomon shut me up in that bottle because I did not obey him. He sealed the top and threw it into the deepest part of the sea. During the first hundred years I said to myself that whoever rescued me would get as much gold as he wanted. In the second hundred years I promised to give all the treasure in the world to my rescuer. But no one opened the bottle. Then I said that my rescuer would become a king and I'd give him three wishes as well. Hundreds of years went by. I was still in the bottle and I fell into a rage. I promised myself that now I would not reward my rescuer but I would kill him. And that is you!"

The fisherman trembled with fear. "Have mercy on me," he begged. But the Genie would not listen. Then suddenly a cunning plan came into the fisherman's head.

"Before you kill me," he said, "will you tell me one thing? Were you really in that little brass bottle?"

"You know that I was."

"Well, I'm not sure about that! Why, not even your hand, let alone a foot, can get inside it. How can you expect me to believe that you can squeeze your body into it?"

"I can do anything I like," said the Genie and he started to growl angrily. "Don't you believe me, wretched man?"

"No, I don't. I won't believe any of the things you have told me either, unless you show me that you can get into that bottle."

He folded his arms and pretended that he was brave but inside he was shaking with fear.

At these words the Genie shook himself and turned into an enormous cloud of smoke. When this cloud almost covered the sea

it started to pour itself little by little into the bottle. Soon the air was clear again and the Genie called out:

"I am back inside as you can hear. Do you believe me now?"

The fisherman did not say a word but he quickly seized the stopper and pushed it into the bottle neck. He screwed it down tightly and then he put the lead seal back on top.

"Now," he shouted joyfully, "it is your turn to beg for your life!"

"Oh please, kind fisherman, let me out. I do not want to stay in this bottle again." The Genie tried to push the stopper and break the seal but he could not manage it. "Let me out," he begged again. "I know that I was unkind to you but I promise never to harm you again. If you let me out, I will make you a rich man."

"No, I do not believe you, so I am going to throw you and the bottle back into the deepest part of the sea. Then I shall tell the other fishermen how ungrateful you were. If they catch this bottle in their nets I shall warn them not to let you out." He picked up the bottle, shook it hard and pretended to throw it away.

The Genie cried out loudly: "I swear that I will keep my word.

May I be killed myself if I break my promise! You will never be poor again; your wife and children will have clothes and plenty of food; you will live in a fine house with a big fishing boat. But you must let me out first!"

The fisherman sat down to think. He wanted to help his family but he did not trust the Genie.

"Will you swear by all the prophets that you will keep your word?" he demanded.

The Genie made a solemn promise which the fisherman knew he would not dare to break so he tugged the stopper out of the bottle. Once more the smoke poured out and went up into the sky. When it came down the Genie stood on the beach and the fisherman shook with fear again. He was more scared still when the enormous Genie kicked the bottle into the sea where it broke into a thousand pieces.

"Do not look so frightened," the Genie said quite kindly, "I made a promise and now I will make you a rich man. Pick up your nets, follow me and do exactly what I tell you."

The Genie led the fisherman to a beautiful lake with four black mountains behind it. There were hundreds of fish swimming in the clear sparkling water but they were very special fish, for each one was coloured either white, yellow, blue or red.

"Cast your nets into the lake," ordered the Genie. "When you pull them in, they will be heavy and filled with fish. You must pick out only four fish, one of each colour."

The fisherman did this and to his surprise there were more fish in his nets than he had ever caught before. He took out one yellow, one white, one red and one blue fish and he threw the rest back.

"Take these fish to the sultan as a present," the Genie said, "he will give you much gold for them. You may come to the lake every day if you wish but you may cast your nets once only and you must never take more than one fish of each colour."

Then the Genie stamped his huge feet. The ground opened and he vanished from sight!

The fisherman took the fish to the sultan at once, who was delighted with the present and rewarded the fisherman handsomely. From that day on the fisherman and his family lived in great comfort and happiness.